Boot Hill Valley

Books by R.G. Yoho

Long Ride to Yesterday
Boot Hill Valley

Kellen Malone Series
Death Comes to Redhawk
Death Rides the Rail

Coming Soon!
Bitter Water
Nightfall Over Nicodemus
The Evil Day
Palo Duro
Return to Matewan
America's History is His Story

For more information
visit: www.SpeakingVolumes.us

Boot Hill Valley

R.G. Yoho

SPEAKING VOLUMES, LLC
NAPLES, FLORIDA
2023

Boot Hill Valley

ISBN 978-1-64540-987-8

I dedicate this book to our country's "Wounded Warriors," men and women who were injured in service to our country. They fight their way back from dreadful injuries and hardships, the likes of which we can only imagine. I know it sounds inadequate, but I thank you so much for your service and sacrifice! America owes you a great debt.

Chapter One

They buried the newly-hired marshal in Boot Hill today.

Nobody who lived in town could ever figure out why the cemetery was called Boot Hill, since it sat in the midst of a long, open valley. To most of the town, it seemed like a real bad place to bury a body.

When the harshest rains fell among the highlands, it wasn't unusual for the remains of several caskets and their bodies to be found floating down the town's main street. Then they had to be buried again, which provided regular and gainful employment for those strong and hardy souls who aspired to make their living bent over a shovel.

Although it was seldom if ever discussed in public, one dead body pretty much looks like the next one. Therefore, a number of its citizens speculated that the remains of their loved ones may not have been re-buried in their original locations, since the only way to identify the dead was by their burial garments, which were often decayed beyond recognition or torn away from their bodies by the roiling flood waters.

The survivors often consoled themselves with the idea that if a mistake in reburial was truly made, at least someone would regularly be kneeling upon or placing flowers on the sod above their loved ones, even it wasn't actually them.

At least they wouldn't be forgotten.

Of course, some of the citizens of Boot Hill Valley were also afraid that, instead of their dearly departed, they might be kneeling down and praying over the body of a thief or murderer who was also buried there. But it was also supposed that a little extra prayer over these blighted souls would certainly do them no lasting harm as they faced the hereafter.

Generally, most people tried not to think about it and trusted the Good Lord, Lucifer, and St. Peter to accurately sort them out for lasting reward or eternal damnation, whichever outcome was most appropriate.

From the hillside, high above Boot Hill, a lonely, young man sat back to watch the proceedings taking place below him. It looked like most everybody in town had come out to attend the marshal's burial.

His boots were off and he was leaning back against a rock, settling in for a long, leisurely drink. Using his teeth to pull loose the cork from the whiskey bottle, he spat the worthless item onto the ground.

A cork's only good for a bottle when something will be left remaining in it.

The funerals were becoming a relatively common occurrence in town, with three different marshals being laid to rest in the past three years.

One of the marshals, after being severely beaten, developed a longing for travel, leaving behind his belongings and a bushel of bad memories. The others were buried in the cemetery down below.

Today's burial would make the fourth, but this was the first time Chance McBride ever took the time to watch the ceremony.

As Chance took a drink, he saw it was almost a majestic sight to behold.

The women were all dressed in black, the men in their Sunday finest. The parson, carrying his black, leather-bound Bible, read from the pages of Scripture, with the sounds of an occasional word or phrase reaching far up to his place upon the hilltop.

The last five marshals had been eager, seemingly-capable men, but somewhat-lacking in the necessary art of gunplay. They were also lacking in the equally-important area of general common sense.

Chance couldn't figure out why anyone would want the job of marshal.

The money was poor; the hours were lousy. And the townspeople were largely ungrateful. It was scarcely worth the danger a man faced for a meager salary of twenty-five dollars a month.

Chance knew . . .

Before these last five souls took the job, he was the town marshal.

They should have learned, Chance thought, *from my bad experiences and scarred hand. The fools should have forked a horse for another town.*

Only one of them had been smart enough to do that.

The sun blistered down from the sky, nearly baking a man's carcass. The men and women dripped sweat inside their heavy, woolen garments.

It had been this way for two months, with no relief and no rain in sight. The heat waves could be seen rising steadily from the ground. The ground was cracked and brittle, leaving gaps in the earth wide-enough to fit a man's thumb. The wind's gentle stirring gave birth to tiny whirlclouds of dust.

Chance took the final pull from his bottle and tossed it on the ground beside him. As it shattered against a rock, a number of heads turned up the hill, facing in the direction of the seemingly-irreverent disturbance.

Upon seeing the drunken, former town marshal, many of them sneered.

Chance ignored their stares, caring about nothing more than the sadness over an empty bottle. The whiskey didn't last as long as it used to. It was getting harder to come by. And it always saddened him to finish off a bottle, as it was about the only friend he had left.

Fortunately, he had another bottle with him.

There was always another.

The difficulty was in acquiring them, a process that often required him to sacrifice whatever few vestiges of dignity he might still hold, since he hadn't yet turned to gaining his liquor by theft.

Once again, he stared down at the funeral and noticed the ones gathering around the casket. Most of the faces were known to him, people who once craved his protection of their lives and businesses.

Now many of them were simply people from whom he begged money, hoping to purchase another bottle. Some of them had been foolish enough to give him a couple bits. Others had looked upon him with disgust and went on their way, shaking their heads at the miserable ruin he made of his life.

Nobody had much use for the town drunk, a wretched, lonely man, given to drink and little else. Chance had become the laughingstock of the town, the object of cruel jokes and remarks, and nobody wished to be seen with him.

Nobody but Amy.

As the crowd began to move away from the gravesite, he stared directly into the eyes of Amy and their eyes held for a moment. Ashamed of his dirty appearance, he quickly looked away, pretending not to notice her stare.

Amy McBride had once been his wife; she was still his wife. But not in any way that truly mattered. They didn't dwell in the same house. They didn't share a bed. The two of them shared only a last name.

Chance walked away from her and immediately crawled into a bottle. And he was certain she didn't need a drunken sot, coming around to embarrass her and further mess up her life.

Amy had been the most lovely woman in Kentucky, a prize to be won and the object of every male suitor in two counties. Chance had to cross the river from West Virginia to win her heart. And she had chosen

4

to marry him, a man with very little in the way of material things to offer.

Chance believed women such as Amy deserved much more than a tin star, a ramshackle house, and a twenty-five dollar a month income.

Amy should have been blessed with a wealthy husband, a spacious house, and many of the finer things in life. And maybe she could have those things now, with him gone from her life. Amy would be free to pursue those things and to finally enjoy the life that God granted her.

But Amy didn't care about any of those things.

As she gazed at the lonely man upon the hillside, her eyes moistened with tears.

In the sparsely assembled crowd of mourners, the tears would largely go unnoticed, appearing as little more than one individual's reasonable expressions of grief over another fallen marshal.

For Amy, it was something else.

To all the world around her, Amy never revealed the pain that burned inside her broken heart. But she was taking full advantage of the situation now.

Amy openly wept, completely releasing her long-restrained feelings of sorrow, fear, and loneliness.

Wiping away the tears from her reddened eyes with a handkerchief, she quickly stole another look up the hillside. Chance stared in her direction, his hard, brown face, darkened from too many hours in the harsh, blistering sun.

His dark and lonely eyes were locked on hers. But it was Chance, who looked away first, unwilling to give into the feelings inside of him.

Chance took another long pull from his bottle.

Seeing Chance again, here, like this, it brought so many memories flooding back to Amy's mind. She remembered the good times they shared, their wedding day and the birth of their child.

She also recalled the bad times, the heartbreaking death of their son. Chance had never quite gotten over it. But in all those times, they always had each other. A loving couple could often make it through anything. But now it was only her, alone.

The sound of singing recaptured her attention, as the crowd lifted their voices in a Gospel hymn. Amy joined in with the singing, her sweet voice blending softly with the others around her.

The sound of their voices made it impossible for them to hear the other sounds, the ones approaching them.

It was then that he first heard it, a soft, low rumble off in the distance.

Chance rose to his feet, searching the horizon for the source of the sound.

At first it was only just the feel of a strong vibration upon the ground. Then it became almost a drumbeat, a sound becoming louder and more ominous.

Then he saw it.

The rumble was the approaching sound of men on horseback, determined men riding fast and hard.

From his vantage point, high above the cemetery, he could see the riders well before they arrived. The men weren't riding like they were racing to attend the burial.

They rode like men intent on causing the burial of several more.

The thought suddenly came to his mind, *Amy's down there.*

The once-precious bottle of whiskey dropped from his hand.

Realizing she might be in danger, Chance knew he must do something.

Unable to quickly locate both his boots, Chance swore softly, starting down the hill in his socked-feet. Shaking off the effects of the alcohol, he stumbled at first, trying to remain upright, desperately seeking to maintain his balance.

His tenuous, stumbling pace grew quicker, a sense of urgency pulling him forward, somehow keeping Chance upright and on his feet.

Hearing the riders growing closer, he broke into a run.

Jagged edges of stones tore into the soles of his feet, as he hurdled over the larger ones. Oblivious to the pain, Chance continued racing down the hill. Sobered by his fear and uncertain of what he was going to do once he got there, Chance increased his speed, running for all the world like Satan's choicest steed.

Once down off the crest of the hill, Chance lost sight of the riders. Now unable to see them and fully determine their whereabouts, the situation made him even more fearful of what might happen to Amy.

Chance knew the riders would be approaching the cemetery at any moment.

There was nothing to do but keep running.

He sprinted down the hill like a man possessed, his hat flying off behind him.

With his legs churning, arms pumping, and lungs bursting, Chance continued running at break-neck speed.

As the team of riders approached the fence around the cemetery, the first shot shattered the arm of a local storekeeper. Bedlam ensued, with startled and angry shouts from the men and shrieks of horror from the ladies.

Horses began pitching and bucking. Men began falling and ducking for cover. And the team of horses that pulled the casket to the cemetery went racing back down the road towards town, without a driver.

Another slug tore through the marshal's pine box, peppering an elderly lady with splinters from the blast. A couple of more shots hit the flowers around the casket, sending their petals flying in all directions.

The guns of the riders claimed the life of one man, quickly followed by another and another. Every trigger pull brought with it the threat of death to another one of the mourners.

Chance approached the cemetery on a dead run, leaping over the fence, and locating Amy. "Get down," he shouted, pushing her to the ground.

As he shielded the woman he loved with his own body, Chance spied a rifle on a nearby horse. The frightened animal was straining hard against his lead reins, which were tied securely to the wheels of a buggy.

Chance knew he'd be lucky to get to the gun without getting shot, but he knew he'd have to try. "Stay down," he shouted to Amy.

Chance rolled over and over upon the ground, scrambled to his feet, and rushed over to catch up the rifle, a gun he could still fire with his one bad hand. Quickly shouldering the weapon, he blasted one of the approaching riders backwards from off his saddle, leaving a bloody path on the horse's hind quarters.

Chance took aim at another and scarcely missed, leaving a bloody stripe down the length of the rider's thigh. He triggered the gun again and again, sending another one of the racing horses back down the trail, riderless.

Chance's unforeseen intervention broke the force of the attack and caused the riders to flee.

Silently, he watched the raiders racing off into the distance.

As the murderous band of horsemen began to ride away, the mourners began to leave their places on the ground, coming to the aid of the wounded and assessing the dead. The attack had been a slaughter, meant to frighten the townspeople away from calling another marshal.

One of the men, after helping his uninjured wife from the ground, looked over Chance from head to toe. His eyes lingered there, a look of disdain on his face.

Uncertain of what the man's look might mean, Chance looked down at himself, realizing the man was staring at his feet. Looking up, he merely shrugged his shoulders about what he was certain must have been a strange sight.

"It's hard to believe we once had this man as our marshal," the man said, taking his wife by the arm. "Come on, Mary. Let's go home."

Another one the men, recognizing the rifle that had been taken from his horse, walked over and snatched away the weapon from the former marshal's hands.

"I'm grateful for what you done here, but you'd only sell it to buy whiskey," he muttered.

As the owner of the rifle departed, Chance walked over and stooped down next to one of the riders he killed. He lifted the man's leg, studied his boot for a moment, and then threw the rider's lifeless limb back down on the ground.

He did take time to snatch up the dead man's hat to replace his own.

Somewhere during this process, Amy had risen from her place of safety. After helping some of the wounded to a waiting buckboard, she began following Chance as he walked amongst the carnage.

Walking over to another dead rider, Chance smiled as he saw the man's boots.

Those look about right.

He stooped down and began pulling the pair of boots from the dead man's feet.

Finding a rare place on the ground that wasn't already marked with fresh blood, Chance chose himself a seat on the ground and began pulling the dead man's boots onto his own feet.

Looking up without shame, his eyes met those of Amy.

"It wasn't like he's going to be needing them anytime soon," Chance said, tugging the boots the rest of the way upon his feet.

After spying another look into the woman's eyes, Chance saw no signs of pity or revulsion at his actions. He saw only love, heartbreak, and a lingering sadness about that which they had lost.

"Amy, dear," one of the women said.

"Yes," she said, flashing one final look at Chance before rushing over to the woman's side.

"Can you help me with my husband, dear? He's been shot."

Amy saw that the wounded man was the local parson.

"Of course," she said, helping the woman get her bloody and wounded husband to a waiting buckboard.

When Amy stole another look where her husband had just been, Chance was already gone, vanishing like a lost and troubled spirit.

* * *

With thoughts of Amy still running through his mind, Chance slowly walked away from the hill overlooking the cemetery. As he wandered by the stream and picked up a rock to toss in the water, he saw his reflection on the surface.

A lean-framed man was standing there, broad of shoulder, and wiry. His face was tough as leather, coarse and hardened by the life he chose for himself.

Chance wasn't very proud of the man who stared back at him. His self-respect was gone, along with his courage and worth as a man. Chance saw himself as a pathetic sight. He was even wearing a dead man's hat and boots.

It was hard to believe that Amy once cared and was willing to share her life with him. But Pete had stolen all of that away from him during the shooting. And despite his best efforts, Chance wasn't able to do anything about it.

A failure.

That's how Chance saw himself. Unable to fight his own battles anymore, now he surrendered to the last one he had left.

Chance took a long glance at his watch, the one with Amy's picture inside the cover. It was the only thing he still owned, the only possession that hadn't been sold to buy whiskey.

Closing the watch and returning it to his battered pocket, Chance continued on his way. Although the trail he followed would take him to the place he lived, it was an aimless and lonely path that was headed anywhere, but led to nowhere.

Chapter Two

Three years ago, Chance and Amy rode their buckboard into the town of Boot Hill Valley. They came from back East, eager to find a better life. This small Colorado community was about as far as their money and patience would get them.

They planned to do some homesteading in this part of the state, planting crops and raising horses. Colorado was a wide open place in those days, with land as far as the eye could see. Their dreams were many and wide as the sunrises.

The very first year, their dreams were instantly destroyed, as a devastating windstorm wiped out almost all of their crops.

Desperate and in need of money, Chance readily accepted the job as town marshal. The money put food on their table and a roof over their heads, but was insufficient to fully restore the dream they once had.

However, Chance never stopped to realize or even imagine how much more that meager salary might ultimately cost him.

Despite its strange name, Boot Hill Valley had once been a peaceful, little town, a fine place to raise crops, horses, and children.

It was Chance's job to maintain order in the town and he took the duties of his badge quite seriously.

But when the Ramseys rode into town, everything changed, and Chance's life was forever altered.

The Ramsey family was made up of three brothers, Pete, Duke, and Jason.

Pete was the oldest of the three and the meanest. Foul-smelling, dirty, and unkempt, he was also the best gun-hand.

Nobody was quite sure how many men he killed, but it was rumored that no less than fifteen men died by Pete's hand.

Duke was nearly as mean as his older brother and a fair hand with a six-shooter himself. But unlike Pete, he fancied himself as a ladies' man. And Duke always made a point to dress for the part.

His clothes were always neat and clean, his boots well-polished. Many of the townspeople found it hard to believe that Duke was Pete's brother. But Duke's natural gravitation towards larceny and murder removed any lingering doubts.

Jason was the youngest of the three and a good boy, for the most part. He was also headstrong and a little on the wild side, like many young men of that age. It was just his misfortune to be saddled with two miserable, no–count varmints for kin.

The Ramseys owned the biggest spread in the area and there was much speculation as to the legality of its acquisition. But most of the speculating was done in hushed tones and whispers.

The previous owner of the ranch had come to an untimely end, thrown from his horse, over a canyon wall . . .

Or so the story goes.

Nobody was willing to say otherwise.

The three brothers also ran the most cattle, mostly because their cows were prolific reproducers, sometimes dropping as many as two to three calves a year. Some also speculated that the Ramsey boys were none too choosy about where they slapped a brand or dapped a loop. But then again, those were just idle rumors, mind you.

The Ramseys had been used to having thing pretty much their own way, but Chance's arrival changed all that.

Law and order was something new in these parts and many folks didn't welcome its arrival with open arms. Differences were settled in other way, fists and six-guns being the most preferred.

For all their troubles with the Ramsey boys, the locals still didn't much cotton to the idea of a town marshal. The people of the West are an independent breed, not prone to giving up their freedoms without a squabble.

And the stranger was new there, green and still wet behind the ears. Despite his skills with a gun, many still thought he had no business wearing a badge.

But Chance took the job anyway.

The first couple of weeks all went pretty much as the young marshal expected.

There were a few minor fights and disagreements, but the towns-people slowly began to trust their young, new marshal and grudgingly accept his presence.

Maybe they even liked having him around.

Then the Ramsey boys rode into town.

* * *

After being on the trail for almost three months, the boys were hankering to live it up. And it wasn't too long before the three brothers crossed paths with the young marshal.

Duke Ramsey was playing stud poker in the Angel's Roost Saloon. He had already won several pots and most of the winnings were in front of him.

One of the players, a young fellow wearing range clothes and a weather-beaten hat, thought he was being cheated. The young man said that Duke was dealing off the bottom, the kind of accusation that often leads to gunplay.

It did this time as well.

When the smoke cleared, the kid was dead on the floor with two bullet holes in the vicinity of his heart.

An unfired gun was found near the stranger's outstretched hands, but he was wearing no holster. And those who knew the young man claimed he never carried a gun.

When McBride charged into the Angel's Roost, he was carrying a double-barrel shotgun, ready for anything he might face inside.

He saw the smiling face of Duke Ramsey, calmly scooping up the winnings and putting them into his pockets.

"What's going on here?" Chance said.

Duke nodded towards the body on the floor. "The kid accused me of cheating and went for his gun. I had no choice but to kill him."

"If that's true, then there'll be no problem." Chance motioned with the barrel of his shotgun. "Come on over to the jail with me,' he said, "until I can get the straight of your story."

Duke bristled at the order. "I ain't going anywhere with you, marshal, especially to jail," he said, looking like he was going for his gun

The double barrel discouraged any of Duke's more foolish notions. "You just unbuckle that gunbelt, stranger. Slowly, with your left hand. Maybe a night in jail will cool you off a little."

"You've got no call to be arresting this man," one of the onlookers said. "It was self-defense and no one in this room will tell you any different."

"Listen, mister. This is law business and it has nothing to do with you."

"That man is my brother. And if you try and put him in jail, marshal, you'll have to answer to me."

"And who might you be?"

"My name is Pete Ramsey."

The name was stated arrogantly, almost defiantly, as if the marshal should be startled by the very sound of it.

"That's a good enough name, I guess. Everybody needs one."

A couple of low snickers could be heard.

Pete's squinty eyes glared at the man. "Are you trying to be funny?"

"No," Chance replied, grinning. "I was just saying that as far as names go, Pete Ramsey isn't anything particularly special."

As the marshal continued his story, Pete observed that the shotgun never even momentarily wavered from his brother's back.

"Come to think of it, I knew a man one time by the name of—what was it? Yes, now I remember. It was Odiferous Osterhage. Yes, sir, now that there's a real name for you. But I guess Pete is acceptable too. Now, if you'll just kindly step aside, I'll just be about my business here."

"And what if I don't?"

"I guess that's a decision you'll have to make for yourself, Mr. Pete Ramsey. But a decision like that might lead to some kind of gunplay," Chance said. "And there's no telling what might happen to your brother if this scatter gun happened to discharge by accident. I'd hate something like that to happen now. Wouldn't you?"

Reluctantly, Pete stepped aside.

"Thank you, sir," he said, sticking the shotgun in Duke's back and prodding him out through the saloon doors.

After they left, Pete stood there in the middle of the saloon, grimly cursing under his breath. "I swear I'll kill that blasted tinhorn."

* * *

After placing Duke in an empty cell, the marshal returned to the Angel's Roost.

16

He talked to all of the available witnesses, but he doubted that any of them were being honest. It was then he came to the conclusion that maybe they were afraid to tell him the truth. Perhaps they were scared of something, or someone.

Chance felt sure that a gun had been placed in the young man's hand, after he was shot. But he had no proof. His simple theories were useless without some evidence to the contrary.

"See, I told you, marshal," Pete said. "Nobody will ever tell you that it was anything other than self-defense."

When Chance saw Ramsey's smug expression, he wanted to take a swing at the man. Despite the ever-growing temptation, he decided it wasn't acceptable behavior for a lawman.

"So, when do you plan to let my brother out of jail?"

"When he failed to simply comply with my order, I charged him with disturbing the peace. Because of that, he'll spend the night in jail. You'll see him in the morning."

In a cynical tone, Chance added," If Duke's in jail, no one will see a need to try and draw on him again. Besides, he's killed enough people for one night." The marshal turned towards the door and paused. "Only one murder per customer."

Rage and hatred washed over his soul as Pete watched Chance push through the saloon doors. He turned to his brother. "That marshal is getting too big for his britches, Jason. It's time we cut him down a notch or two."

"What do you plan to do about him, Pete?"

"I don't know yet, but whatever I decide, the doing of it will be a pleasure."

* * *

17

When morning came, the pair of brothers were waiting just outside the jail.

It pained Chance to release Duke, but he had no other choice. He couldn't keep a man in jail for self-defense, even if he was certain it didn't actually happen that way.

There were no witnesses—at least none willing to testify.

Duke's head rested on his hands, staring at the ceiling as he lay stretched out on the rickety, old, steel cot. He looked up quickly when he heard the key turning in the lock.

"You're free to go, Duke," Chance said, handing over the man's gunbelt, "but you'd be better off getting out of town for a while."

While strapping back on his gun, he replied," "I'll go when I'm good and ready, marshal.

The look on Ramsey's face was taunting and self-satisfied.

It was almost more than Chance could stand.

"If you don't wipe that smirk off your face, I'll do it for you."

While walking towards the door, Duke paused and turned, like he was debating whether or not to draw on the lawman.

Facing him were the dark, twin barrels of McBride's scatter gun.

"I really wish you would, Duke. At this range, my shotgun would cut you in half."

The man started to leave.

"One more thing, Duke."

"What's that?"

"If you kill another person in Boot Hill Valley, I'll see that you swing for it. Now, get out of here, Duke, while I still remember I'm a peace officer."

Pete and Jason waited outside, smiling as Duke came out the door. Pete slapped him on the back and said, "Let's get a drink."

"Isn't it a little early for that?"

"Not for us," Pete said, throwing an arm around his brother's shoulders. "We've been out here all night."

On their way to the saloon, the Ramsey brothers passed Amy. She was walking down the street, coming to meet Chance, when their paths crossed.

Pete's eyes followed her, savoring her lovely face and form. "A woman who looks like that one shouldn't waste herself on a man like McBride."

Amy ignored Pete's comment as if she didn't hear it and continued walking.

From across the street, Chance had seen the whole thing take place before him. Anger rose in his soul. And for one brief moment, he knew.

This dispute he had with Pete Ramsey would never end peaceably.

* * *

For the next couple of days, Boot Hill Valley was peaceful and without incident. But conditions soon changed . . .

Jason Ramsey got in a fight at the saloon and Chance rushed over to stop the brawl. But his generally-good, common sense had been altered by his libations.

Then he took a swing at McBride.

It would be several hours before Jason would regain consciousness, the newest guest of the city, stuck behind iron bars.

The door swung open and Pete barged into Chance's office. "I want to see my brother now."

"Sure thing," Chance said. "Just leave your gunbelt out here first."

"I'm not giving up my gun."

"That's your right, Pete, but you're not going back there with it."

"You had no call to arrest Jason. All he did was get into a fight."

"And had he not chosen to take a poke at me, his carcass wouldn't be back there rotting in a cell."

Pete's eyes filled with hatred, more hatred than Chance had ever seen in another man. "One of these days, you're going to cut too wide a swath. And when that happens, I'll be right there, spitting tobacco juice on your miserable hide."

"I don't like threats, Pete. Now get out of here, before you join your brother."

"I'm leaving, but not before I give you a warning. I'll get you, McBride, if it's the last thing I do. You'll pay for messing with us. I swear it."

Pete turned swiftly and headed for the door.

As his boot hit the street, a plan began to form in his mind. Tonight, he would get Jason out of jail and get even with McBride.

The marshal is finally going to get what he has coming.

* * *

The sun was just beginning to set over the mountains as Chance finished his daily rounds and headed home for dinner.

His lips whistled a tune, keeping time with the jingling of his spurs. The wind carried a faint scent of dinner, growing stronger as he came nearer to the house. It was then he realized how hungry he'd become and longed to get back home.

Stepping out from between the buildings were Pete and Duke Ramsey.

Pete's green, tobacco-stained teeth were bared in a vicious smile. His dirty, tattered clothes were in strong contrast to his brother's appearance.

Duke was dressed in his Sunday finest, white shirt, black coat, and well-polished boots. His hat was worn down low and his cold, deadly eyes peered at the marshal from underneath the brim.

Realizing that he didn't share the speed of a Luke Short or Ben Thompson with a six-gun, McBride generally carried a rifle or a shotgun. On this day he had neither. He realized that his hurry to get to supper had caused him to foolishly leave it behind.

Pete smiled as he noticed its absence. "I see you ain't got your long gun, marshal. It's dangerous to forget a thing like that, especially with all the enemies you've got."

Chance's mind labored feverishly, looking for some kind of an edge, some way to live out the evening. But he saw none.

Pete spoke again. "You never know what kind of trouble could be waiting for a man."

"You've got a point, Pete. Wait right here for me and I'll go get it. Be right back."

"Isn't he a funny one? You hear that, Duke? The marshal has a sense of humor."

Duke simply nodded, the gun already in his hand.

Chance knew Pete planned to kill him, but he wanted to savor it first, enjoying the moment to its fullest. "I've been wondering. Just how good are you with that six-shooter?" Pete said, looking over at his brother. "He sure isn't saying much, is he, Duke?"

Duke didn't respond, but he smiled at the remark.

"I reckon," Pete continued, "some folks talk a lot more when they have the upper hand, sticking a shotgun in your back."

The two of them continued to taunt the marshal, hoping McBride would eventually beg for his life. Chance would have no part of it.

"Maybe he's just a coward, Duke. He sure don't rile easy."

The Ramsey brothers planned to push Chance into a fight and then kill him. And the marshal knew there would be no way of getting around it and it was doubtful that he could count on any help.

If a fight couldn't be avoided, Chance decided he would choose the moment.

"What do you think, Duke? Don't you figure his wife wonders what a real man would be like?"

The words burned his soul like hot iron on a calf's hind quarters. His hand clawed for his gun.

It cleared the holster in a heartbeat, but came a second too slowly.

Pete's first shot burned the marshal's chest and he turned with the impact.

Although his draw hadn't been fast enough to beat the older brother, Chance put a slug into Duke's shoulder before he could trigger his first shot. Another one buckled the brother's leg.

Knowing Pete was the most dangerous of the two, Chance turned his gun on Pete just as another slug struck him.

He struggled to keep his balance and winced from the searing pain in his chest. He triggered the gun and its shot blew off the top of Pete's ear.

Chance's ears exploded with the sound of roaring six-guns and he was hit, again and again. The gun dropped from his hand and the shooting stopped. He felt something dripping onto his boot.

As the marshal bent over to stare at the ever-growing red puddle, the ground rose to meet him.

He rolled over, trying to get to his feet. Looking up, Pete and Duke towered above Chance's fallen body and he stared into their deadly eyes.

The words came slowly, as spasms of pain swept through the marshal's body. "Why don't you just finish me off, Pete?"

Pete spat a stream of tobacco juice into the marshal's face. "Let him lay there and die slow." As an afterthought, he said, "You need to be taught that you don't pull iron on a Ramsey."

And with a smile, he triggered his gun once again and sent a slug through Chance's right hand.

After their final act of contempt, Pete and Duke headed for the jail to free their brother, Jason.

As Chance was sprawled out in the dusty street, he fought back the pain and struggled to remain conscious. Thinking only of Amy, he once again tried to rise. His dinner would be getting cold and Amy would be angry with him.

The pain began to subside and Chance's thoughts became twisted, meaningless ideas and darkness finally closed upon him.

Chapter Three

A lawman's wife lives with one fear above all others, that her husband will be killed in the performance of his duties, the unfortunate victim of a shooting. This terror is always in back of the woman's mind. And although it may never be spoken, it is seldom if ever forgotten.

Amy McBride heard the gunshots in the street and rushed to her window, afraid that her greatest fear was being realized.

Her heart became gripped with fear and panic, as she saw the two gunmen walking away from Chance's motionless body.

Charging out of the door of her house, Amy sprinted to her fallen husband's side. She sobbed uncontrollably as the town folk began to rush in all around her.

"Chance has been shot. Someone get the doctor," she shouted. "Hurry!"

Amy knelt beside him, resting his head in her arms, Chance's blood staining her dress. She couldn't understand why anyone would want to hurt her husband.

"Please don't die," she pleaded.

Doc Arnold was there in a matter of minutes and ordered the spectators to stand back. "Give the man some room," he said.

Amy wept openly as the doctor examined the wounded lawman. "A couple of you men, help me carry him back to my office."

A pair of large men stepped out from among the crowd and carried the marshal's body to Doc Arnold's office. They brought him inside the office and carefully placed him down on the doctor's table.

"I need you to wait outside," Arnold said.

"No," she said. "I'm not going anywhere."

With only one look in her eyes, the doctor saw that there was no reason in trying to argue with the woman. "Okay, then go and get me those towels out of that drawer over there."

Doc Arnold immediately began to go to work on the man, stripping away his bloody shirt and bathing his wounds. Then for the next three hours, Amy watched as the doctor gruelingly labored to remove several slugs from the marshal's body.

"Do you think he will live?" Amy said, as the doctor finished binding up her husband's wounds.

"It's too early to tell, dear."

The aged doctor rose from his place next to the bed. He removed a handkerchief from his coat pocket and wiped the perspiration from his forehead.

"The next few hours will be very critical."

Amy moved her chair closer to her husband's side and carefully took his hand.

Placing a gentle hand on the frightened wife's shoulder, he said, "I've done about everything I can do for him. It's up to him now. And God."

Arnold ran a hand through his diminishing strands of silvery hair. "The boy is strong," he added, hoping to bring some comfort to her. "Why don't you go home and get some sleep? I'll stay here with him and let you know if his condition changes."

Amy smiled sweetly. "Thank you anyway, doctor, but I'd prefer to remain here."

"Of course, you're welcome to do as you wish, Mrs. McBride. I suppose he'll be in good hands then. So, if you'll excuse me, I'd like to go have a drink and a bite to eat."

Arnold closed his black, leather bag and began to leave.

"Doctor," Amy said, "thank you."

He paused in the doorway. "My pleasure, dear. I hope it's been enough."

Amy remained by her husband's side thoughout the endless hours of the night. She didn't sleep much, only taking brief naps which were often interrupted by her man's labored breathing.

When Chance became fevered, she mopped his brow with cold, damp cloths. When he began to shiver, she would place another blanket upon him to remove the chill. And no nurse could have given him any better care than she, a concerned and loving wife.

Just before daylight, when it seemed that the worst of the ordeal was over, Amy finally drifted off to sleep.

She was awakened by a gentle tap on her arm.

Amy smiled as she noticed Chance staring at her from off his pillow.

"For a little while there," she said, "I thought I had lost you."

"No such luck," he said, scarcely above a whisper. "You can't get rid of me that easily."

About that time, Doc Arnold walked in the door. "I must be a much better doctor than I realized," he said. The doctor shook his head in astonishment, constantly surprised by mankind's often-stubborn will to survive."I didn't really expect you to live out the night."

Amy looked mortified by the doctor's remark, but Chance merely smiled. "You sure know how to build up a man's confidence in the medical profession, Doc. But it doesn't make any difference. I'm too mean and ornery to throw good dirt over."

The doctor glared at him."You're lucky to be alive, son. I removed several slugs from you last night and you lost a ton of blood." He pulled another chair next to the bed and sat down. "One of those slugs was only inches away from your heart."

For the first time, Chance noticed the bandage on his right hand. He had forgotten about being shot there, thinking it only to have been a bad dream. Fighting back the pain it caused to move, he raised his arm in front of his eyes to survey the damage.

"Doc," he said, "how is my hand? How is it really?"

Arnold hesitated for a moment, searching for the proper choice of words. But he could think of none. "I'm not going to pull any punches with you, marshal. Your hand was severely wounded and you may never regain the total use of it. I'm not saying it is impossible, but it is unlikely. But only time will tell."

"Who needs a marshal who can't use a gun?" Chance said. "They should have just killed me."

Amy's head turned suddenly at the remark, her eyes blazing in anger. "What about me, Chance? You think I would be better off? Don't you understand that I need you here? I don't want to ever hear you say anything like that again."

"Perhaps one of those big city doctors, like you'd likely find in Chicago, could do you more good than I ever could," said Doc Arnold. "I just don't have the skills you need."

Amy interrupted their conversation. "That's enough talk for now," she said. "It's time for the good doctor to leave and for you to get some more rest."

Doc Arnold smiled sheepishly and said, "Yes, doctor."

He said nothing more and hustled through the door.

"Your bedside manner needs some work," Chance said.

"And that will be enough out of you, Mr. McBride. You need to sleep."

In no time at all, the marshal drifted back to sleep.

* * *

A couple of weeks later, Chance was moving around much better and ready to go back to work.

Then the news came.

Boot Hill Valley was going to hire a new marshal.

After the shooting, the townspeople had been outraged about the incident, but as Chance recovered, their initial sense of anger was soon forgotten. And the Ramsey brothers stayed away from the town until things calmed back down.

A few of the people had wanted the outlaws punished, but their number had been relatively small. And who would have the courage or the wherewithal to bring them in for trial?

Out of fear for leaving behind a grieving widow, nobody had stepped forward, willing to brace the brothers with a gun. Old age and fear had prevented any retaliation or justice on the marshal's behalf.

Doc Arnold had been one of the town's most outspoken citizens and stated that the brothers ought to be jailed and stand trial.

At a town meeting, Arnold was the only one to speak his peace boldly, when he said, "The shooting on a lawman isn't only a senseless act of violence; it is also a savage attack on an orderly, law-abiding society. Incidents such as these must never be tolerated."

The three Ramsey brothers walked into the saloon, where the meeting was being held, during the midst of Arnold's speech. And although he made note of their entrance, he changed not a single word of his silver-tongued oratory.

When the outlaws' presence was realized, some of the townspeople began to filter out of the room, fearing that they might incur the brothers' anger. Most of the others remained, unwilling to be driven away.

Arnold knew that his speech would stir their hatred and contempt for him. Perhaps it might also cost him his life. But that realization made no difference to him. He believed that truth needed to be declared, no matter what the cost. The Ramsey brothers' presence only served to fuel the flames of determination, which burned inside his soul.

"We need to band together," Arnold said, "and drive these outlaws from our midst. For if we do nothing, we are not fit to call ourselves men."

Many of the locals agreed with the doctor's speech, but they failed to do anything about it. Few of them were willing to go against the Ramsey brothers in anything.

Pete stood there silently, listening to those things being said, also taking a mental note of those who failed to leave. And when everyone had spoken his peace, he decided that it was his turn.

Climbing on top of the bar, he began, "Since this happens to be a town meeting, I want to put in my palaver too."

Pete paused long enough to watch the reaction of the crowd and then rubbed his hollow, unshaven jaws.

"Me and my brothers bring a lot of business into this town and we don't take kindly to being treated like outlaws. A town's leading citizens should be treated with a heap more respect. We also don't cotton to having our kin tossed into jail by your latest tin-horn marshal."

He quit speaking long enough to lean over and pour himself a drink of whiskey, which he held as he continued to talk.

"From now on," he said, "we're going to do whatever we want. If we want something, we'll just take it. That means whiskey, food, supplies at the general store." Pete paused suddenly and looked directly at Amy, a vile, sinister gaze that chilled her soul and made her feel dirty and uncomfortable. "And anything else we want."

Ramsey finished his whiskey in a single gulp and tossed the glass across the saloon, shattering it against the wall and striking a number of the townspeople with its remains.

"If you or anybody else tries to stop us, you'll end up like that glass. We'll break you. There now; I've about said what I come to say. Go ahead and finish your meeting now. Good day to you and we'll be seeing you all soon," Pete said, a devilish smirk resting on his face.

Pushing through the now-silenced crowd, he went out the door, followed closely by his brothers, Duke and Jason.

"So, there you have it," Doc Arnold said, recapturing the crowd's attention. "Do you want a town run by outlaws? Do you want a town where a decent lady can't walk down the streets safely, even in broad daylight? That's not for me! We have to stand behind our marshal and help in any way we can, even if it means taking up arms ourselves."

"But what about McBride?" someone in the crowd shouted. "Some folks are saying that he can't even use a gun anymore."

"Yes, that's right for now," Arnold said.

Another man added, "If McBride can't do the job, I say we call someone who can."

Many of the townspeople agreed with the speaker and voiced their support with shouts and murmurs. Refusing to believe that they would turn their backs on her husband and visibly shaken by the events that had taken place in the saloon, Amy rushed out the door.

When the news reached McBride, he was not surprised by the town's decision. It had been expected. The townspeople were understandably afraid. And if there was to be any justice for the shooting, Chance would have to do it himself.

The doctor came by their house later, to check on McBride's hand and to express his regrets for what happened in the meeting. "I had no idea that any of this would happen," Arnold replied, as he examined Chance's hand.

"I don't blame them," said Chance. "Except for Pete coming to interrupt the meeting, I already knew how it would go. That's why I wasn't there. They're afraid, Doc. Who wouldn't be? And what good is a marshal who can't use a gun?"

"They still shouldn't call another marshal, at least not until you had a chance to prove you couldn't do the job," Amy said.

"The hand has healed nicely, but you'll need to try to use it," the doctor explained. "I'm sorry about the way things turned out, Chance. I really am."

Chance nodded.

"Well, I must go now. Make sure that you exercise that hand every day, but don't push it too hard at first."

"Are you sure that you can't stay for a cup of coffee?" Amy asked.

"Yes, I'm sure. Mrs. Fields is expecting soon and I must stop in and check on her. Good afternoon," Arnold said, as he closed the door behind him.

After Arnold left, Chance picked up his gun. It just didn't feel right in his grasp. He could no longer ear back the hammer with his thumb and his finger couldn't manage to reach the trigger properly. After several tries, in disgust, Chance gave up.

Sadly, Amy watched as her husband worked with the gun. It hurt her deeply to see him in this condition. But Amy was also torn. She wanted him back to normal, but feared what might happen to Chance should he be forced to confront the brothers again.

She fought back the tears that seemed to be welling up inside of her.

For the next two weeks, Chance worked with the gun every day. But there had been no improvement. With each try, there came failure.

And with each failure, there came disappointment. McBride even tried to draw with his left hand, but that hadn't been much better either.

It wasn't long before Chance turned to the bottle, in order to forget.

Like any wife, Amy noticed the change in her husband, but she was powerless to do anything to help. All of her attempts to talk with him had been rejected and he refused to admit there was a problem. With each day, the drinking consumed more and more of the man he'd once been.

The drinking became even worse when the new marshal arrived and it grew when Pete and Duke Ramsey murdered him. And when that lawman died, another part of Chance McBride died with him. It was then that Chance moved out of the house, to the abandoned lineshack.

For the next three years, Chance continued to drink, seldom thinking about the woman he married. And when he did think of her, it made him want to drink more.

McBride believed that he failed at everything, the death of his son, the inability to use his hand, and the weeks and months of drunkeness. All of these things convinced Chance that he was worthless and somehow undeserving of the love Amy had given him.

Because he'd been able to do nothing to protect the town, Chance considered himself to be a failure as a man. Several of its citizens had been killed or harmed, along with the marshals who had been murdered by the outlaws.

McBride believed that if he'd been able to use a gun, then no harm would have needed to come to any of them. And in order to forget, Chance drank.

McBride sold his gun and saddle. He also sold a large portion of his soul, in order to buy the whiskey he craved. Nothing was important to Chance anymore, nothing but the whiskey.

And Amy.

Chapter Four

Chance arrived back at the line shack, tired from the events at the cemetery. His throat was dry and he began searching for the bottle that he'd earlier hidden away.

Seeing Amy at the graveside had brought back too many painful, old memories. She was still as lovely as the first day they met. With enough whiskey, he hoped to forget about this day. Maybe he could even forget about her.

He took a drink and doubted it would be enough.

In a far corner of a small, lopsided cabinet, he found the hidden bottle. It was a welcomed sight. He pulled at the cork with his teeth and spat it across the tiny room. Throwing his neck all the way back, Chance took a long, deep swig from it. The whiskey burned all the way down, as it exploded into his stomach.

Just as he was beginning to feel its first effects, there was a low knock on the door. And since it was generally uncommon for folks to mingle or visit with the town drunk, he was startled at the sound of it.

Fear or surprise, or a combination of them both, caused him to drop his precious bottle. The neck of the bottle broke off and the whiskey began to pour out on the floor. And knowing that it was the last of his supply, Chance scrambled onto the floor, hoping to save some of it.

Alcohol had become his entire life and nothing was more important than saving his booze. While still in his haste to rescue the spilled liquor, he forgot about the knock on the door.

As he crawled on the floor, fumbling with the broken glass, another knock could be heard. The disturbance now bothered him and he cursed the interruption of the mission at hand. He hoped they would get tired and go away.

But the unknown visitor was persistent and rapped on the door once again. Disgusted and impatient, he finally answered, "Come on in, dammit."

Still trying to salvage his bottle, Chance never stopped to look up.

The door opened slowly, almost tentatively.

"Hello, Chance," the visitor said.

The voice was a familiar one and he recognized it immediately. The very sound of the words tugged at Chance's heart and sent icy fingers down his spine.

It was Amy.

As he looked up, he found himself staring into a lovely pair of hazel eyes, the most beautiful ones he'd ever seen. Then he remembered that he was on the floor, on his hands and knees, frantically trying to save some spilled whiskey.

Chance could only imagine how pathetic he might look to someone at that moment.

"It was good to see you again, Chance," she said, smiling and unsure of what to say. "And thank you for helping me today. You saved my life."

His heart beat faster at the sweet sound of Amy's lovely voice. He tried to say something in response, but his mouth was suddenly dry and the words caught in the back of his throat.

Amy continued to stand in the doorway. "May I come in?" she said.

Embarrassed by his lack of good manners to someone he still loved, Chance replied, "Of course. I'm sorry. Please come on in."

"Thank you."

"Would you care to sit down, Amy?" he said, brushing the dust off the least-battered chair in the room. This he placed behind her and held it while she sat.

"Thank you, Chance."

Chance returned another broken chair to an upright position and sat down next to the woman.

Amy stared at the man sitting across from her, as though she was seeing him for the first time. His mannerisms hadn't changed and his face still looked the same, except for an extra line or two.

She thought of the day they were married and remembered how much in love they had been. Amy certainly missed those days.

Things were different between the two of them now, but the strong feeling she possessed for her husband had not changed. In spite of his weakness and the disgrace that Chance brought to her, Amy still loved him fiercely.

Time had done nothing to change that.

She suspected that deep down inside, Chance probably still felt the same.

Chance sat there in front of her, wanting to say something, but small talk didn't seem appropriate. Finally able to think of anything else to say, he blurted out, "How are you doing, Amy?"

It was a stupid question to ask and he hated himself for actually uttering the words.

How could she be?

The woman had been left alone for three years, deserted by her drunken husband. The man had disgraced her on almost a daily basis, by hanging around town and begging for drinks. And Chance recognized it was a mighty foolish question.

"I've been all right," she replied, all the while knowing she was deliberately lying to the man. "Some days are better than others."

Knowing that Amy had never been one to accept charity, Chance suddenly found himself wondering how she managed to get by. After being so wrapped up in his sense of self-pity, the thought never crossed his mind before. It shamed him now because it finally did.

Chance hung his head.

Amy had just came from the burial and was dressed in dark clothing, which Chance always thought looked good on her.

For the first time in months, Chance gave some thought to his own appearance. He knew he didn't much resemble the man she married, but now, he was both happy and ashamed to be in the same room with her.

Chance's face showed several days growth of beard and he wished he could have shaved before she saw him this closely. He hoped Amy didn't notice as he tried to brush some of the dirt off his scroungy range clothes. Nervously, like a youngster first going courting, Chance ran his fingers through his hair, trying to comb out its dark, tangled strands.

"I'd offer you a drink," he said, "but I don't really have something fit for a lady."

"That is fine, Chance, I'm not really thirsty anyway."

Looking deeply into her eyes, Chance saw something that troubled him. There was a hesitation as she spoke, like she was holding back some critical piece of information.

No longer able to rein in his curiosity, he said, "What can I do for you, Amy?"

Amy paused for a moment, as if searching for the proper words to say. "I told myself that I wouldn't come to you for help. I also swore I wouldn't be a bother to you, Chance."

"You're not a bother to me."

With a wave of her hand, Amy cut him off before he could say anything else. "Stop it, Chance. Wait. I need to say this to you now, before I lose my nerve.

"I swore to myself that I would leave you alone, that I wouldn't trouble you. And I tried, Chance. I really did. But today at the cemetery, after seeing you come to my aid, I just can't do it anymore." Tears began welling up in her eyes. "So, I just have to say it. I need your help. I'm scared, Chance."

Her reply came as a total shock to him, leaving a drunken man, coldly sober.

When she started speaking, Chance expected her to say that she was leaving Boot Hill Valley, anxious to return to her family and also to escape the shame his behavior brought down upon her.

But he never expected this, a cry for help.

A cry to him.

"What's got you scared, Amy?"

In all their years of married life, Amy had always been a strong, courageous woman. For that quality alone, any man would have been proud of her.

She had never been one to be frightened easily, spooked by every little noise or unexplained movement. If Amy was scared of something or someone, then Chance knew there had to be a good reason for it.

The answer came quickly, without pause or hesitation. "I'm scared of Pete Ramsey."

The very mention of Pete's name sent a flood of hatred through Chance's soul.

Chance's drinking, their separation, Pete had been responsible for all that happened with them.

At that moment, Chance longed to kill Pete Ramsey, to shoot him down and walk away, the same way Pete had done with him.

"How long has this been going on?"

"For quite some time now," she said.

Looking deeply into her eyes, the ones that revealed the things her lips would never say, Chance saw only rage and fear.

"Why didn't you tell me this was going on earlier?"

Amy was hesitant to answer, looking for the proper words. She couldn't find them.

"I thought you had enough problems of your own." Amy swallowed hard. "And you just haven't been around much."

His head hung low at her reply, the words cutting deeply, like a sharp knife piercing his soul.

Amy was right; he hadn't been around much. He had forsaken the only woman who ever cared for him and turned to the bottle, yielding to the terrible weakness inside of him, the liquor enslaved him. And until now, he was simply unwilling to give it up.

"Do you remember the way Pete used to look at me?" Amy asked. Not waiting for his response, she continued, "Lately, he's done more than that, making several evil advances towards me.

"They are gone now, off on a trail drive. But when they return, Pete plans to take me to his ranch. He told me so." Her eyes suddenly softened. "Chance," she said, "I'm scared of that animal."

This had been going on for these many months and Chance was completely unaware of it. Swallowed up in self-pity, he was blind to the troubles around him, most of all to those faced by his wife.

He realized his problems seemed small and insignificant when compared to those Amy experienced. Chance only hoped Amy could somehow forgive him.

Amy spoke again, timidly asking the question that had been preying on her mind since she first arrived at the shack.

"Chance, would you come back home?" Still unsure of what his answer might be, she quickly added, "If only to protect me from Pete Ramsey."

Amy knew that Chance hadn't changed. And despite the troubles with the bottle, his courage was still intact. As long as the man still drew a breath, she knew he would never allow any harm to come her way.

Even though her man had gone away for a time, the womanly part of her recognized that he still cared. Chance might appear slightly different on the outside, but underneath that calloused exterior, Amy still sensed the same tenderness she once knew.

"You know I'd never willingly let anything happen to you, Amy," he said, turning from her to face the back wall. "But what makes you so sure I can even do anything to protect you, Amy? My gun hand is still damaged. You and I both know that I'm no match for Pete or Duke."

Amy walked over to her husband, placing her hand on his shoulder and turning him around to face her. "What other choice to I have?" she said. "I saw you today at the cemetery. I saw you come running off that hillside to protect all of us. To protect me.

"Listen, Chance. No matter what condition you might be in, I'm not scared to face whatever might happen if you're there beside me.

"Sure, I'll come back if you still want me."

Amy beamed. "I've never wanted anything more."

Chance and Amy embraced in the middle of the tiny lineshack, joyously reunited.

They spent the rest of the afternoon together, talking, laughing, and enjoying each other's company. With her there beside him again, Chance even forgot about his immediate desire for the whiskey. The hours passed so swiftly, the two of them hadn't realized that it was nearly evening.

"Come on. Let's go home, Chance."

"Home, that word sure has a nice ring to it." he said, following his wife out the door. Remembering that he had no horse, he paused just outside the door.

Seemingly, Amy already knew what he was thinking. "I brought an extra horse with me," she said proudly.

"Doggone sure of yourself, weren't you?"

Amy nodded.

While he checked the cinch on his saddle, Amy mounted up.

He leaned on the saddle and said, "I won't be much help to you, Amy. I don't even own a gun anymore."

Without speaking, she quickly reached into her saddlebags and handed Chance a holstered six-gun.

The pistol butt was made of dark walnut and it had recently been polished, shining like it was brand new. Looking it over carefully, he recognized it immediately as being his, the one he sold to buy whiskey.

"Where did you get this?" he said. "I never figured to see it again."

"I purchased it from the man you sold it to, but he wouldn't part with the saddle."

He smiled at her. "You sure thought of everything."

Amy, smiling from ear to ear, reined her horse around. "Yes, I did."

As they headed for home, they set a steady, easy-going pace. Amy and Chance were in no hurry and there were no deadlines which needed to be kept. Nobody was expecting them, so they moved along slow, enjoying each other's company once again.

On their way back to the house, they didn't travel the main road. Caution had always been a habit of his and the old ways often die hard. To the best of his knowledge, Chance didn't believe they were in any immediate danger, but the townsfolk at Boot Hill thought the same thing, until the riders came. It never hurt to be too careful.

The night was clear and perfect. It was what the Texans call a Comanche Moon. With the moon and stars illuminating all the things below them, the raiding parties would attack and steal from the settlers.

A wolf's lonely and mournful howl echoed in the hills and the noisy crickets sang their happy tune.

Chance and Amy were surrounded by the uninterrupted, peaceful sounds of the night. These were sounds that Chance had grown accustomed to and their normal presence was a welcomed reassurance of a man's immediate safety.

During their ride to the house, they had eventually become a part of the night. Theirs had been a peaceful ride and the creatures of the dark had accepted their presence.

When a man enters the wilderness, he becomes an intruder, an uninvited guest into the home of another. If that same man remains there, blending in with his surroundings and creating no further danger or disturbance, the wilderness will finally accept him as being one with itself.

Deer and many other creatures will largely ignore a man's presence if they sense that man is no immediate threat to their well-being.

It's the same way with the night. Once a man's intrusion has been accepted, then he and the night may become as one.

Chance was pleased that he and Amy were back together and he softly cursed himself for the time he'd wasted. He knew he'd been a fool. A man's life is short, but no matter what his end might eventually turn out to be, he ought to live it with the ones he holds dear. Never again would he forget.

The gentle, evening breeze had a slightly warm tinge to it. Chance's horse ambled along steadily and he enjoyed the feeling of freedom it gave him.

Suddenly, the peaceful sounds of the evening vanished. All that remained was the gentle, evening breeze and a subtle warning of danger.

When those noises subsided, every one of Chance's nerves went on edge, trying to sense what the danger might be.

No man should ever disregard his instincts, for they are the senses that warn him of coming hazards which are often unseen. And over the years, Chance's instincts had often been the only things which kept him alive.

The sounds of the night do not change without a mighty good reason. Something out of the ordinary was taking place and the creatures all around them had been disturbed by it.

Motioning his wife to stay behind, Chance dismounted his horse and crept over to a clump of bushes. As he peered through the midst of them, his ears straining to hear, the cause for alarm soon became apparent. What he saw was enough to make a man's hair stand on end.

A lynching was about to take place.

One tough-looking character was placing a noose around the neck of an Indian, while another stranger stood watch with a gun.

The Indian looked to be many years old and weathered. But even while facing imminent death, the Indian was firm and stoic.

Although Chance always believed in minding his own business, he was also a great believer in fair play. The odds certainly weren't in the old Indian's favor, so he figured he would just even them up a mite.

He motioned to Amy, who climbed down and quietly looked the situation over also. She leaned over closer to Chance as he whispered a plan into her ear.

"Be careful," she whispered.

"You too."

Amy nodded in agreement, moved to her horse, and removed the rifle from its scabbard. Then she chose another position from which she could see and gain a good field of fire.

The old Indian was sitting astride his horse, hands tied behind his back. It was likely he'd once been a great warrior, for he made no effort to fight the rope, remaining strong and silent in the face of death.

The two men were just about to slap the horse on the rump, which would cause the horse to run out from under the Indian, leaving his feet to dangle off the ground. So, if he was going to do something, Chance knew this was the time.

Cocking the gun with his left hand, Chance quietly slipped through the bushes, six-gun in hand. As he pointed his gun at the would-be hangmen, he said, "If you've got plans on hanging this Indian, you might want to reconsider.

Holding the gun in his bad hand, Chance knew he wouldn't have much of a shot if they chose to shoot it out. But with Amy as the Ace up his sleeve, he hoped to run a bluff on the strangers.

Their faces could be clearly seen in the brightness of the Comanche Moon and they were none too pleased that someone interrupted their festivities. Neither of them looked familiar and Chance was sure he didn't know them.

The moonlight flashed off his six-gun and they noticed it for the first time. Their smug looks of pleasure and self-confidence faded upon seeing the gun.

The one who put the noose around the Indian's neck was a hard-looking individual with a scar under his left eye. He had the look of a man who'd seen a lot of miles, most of them dodging the law.

Chance figured him to be the meanest one of the two.

The other man was a bearded rascal, with red hair and crazy eyes. He had holstered his gun just before Chance appeared. Now his hand twitched above the pistol butt, as if he wanted to draw.

The meanest one of the two said, "You'd best mind your own business, stranger. This is none of your affair."

"Maybe so," Chance said, "but Im making it my business."

"This here Injun is ours," the other man said. "We caught him fair and square. But you're welcomed to have him, or whatever's left of him, just as soon as we've had our fun."

"I like a little fun myself, every now and again, but yours is over for tonight." Chance tipped the gun slightly, pointing it right at the bearded one's brisket. It was clear to Chance that the man didn't like it one bit. "Now cut the Indian loose!"

The one nearest to the Indian, with the scar under his eye, glared in his direction. "Are you some kind of an Indian lover?" he asked.

"No, I'm not. I'm just a man with a loaded six-gun and a bad temper and my patience is beginning to run a little thin."

Chance had just about worked his bluff to the limit and it was clear they were getting notions about going for their guns. But Amy had been watching closely and she quickly levered a shell up into the chamber.

At the sound of Amy's rifle, they realized Chance was not alone.

The bearded one swallowed hard, not really wanting to tackle a pair of gunmen.

Chance leveled his gun at the man with the scar. "Cut him loose. Now."

He reached behind the Indian's back and sliced the rope off his wrists. His next move, by the sheer swiftness of it, nearly caught Chance off guard.

With a nearly-blinding move of the hand, the man swept the hat from his head, viciously striking the horse on the rump.

The startled horse bolted from underneath the Indian.

Fortunately, the brave's hands had been cut free and they clung to the rope above his head. He dangled at the end of a hangman's noose, eyes wide, hanging on for his own life.

The sudden turn of events did not surprise Amy. She took careful aim and squeezed off a shot from the rifle . . .

As soon as he struck the horse, scar eye clawed for his gun. The revolver cleared leather and its slug barely missed Chance's left side.

He never got another shot, because Amy's heavy, rifle slug struck him then, thrusting his body into the trunk of the hanging tree.

His eyes filled with shock and horror, as he clutched at his chest, pulling away a bloody hand. The gun had fallen from his now-useless fingers and it seemed like a dozen miles away from him. As the man with the scar grasped for it, he slumped over on his face, silent and unmoving.

The bearded one's face took on a dreadful look of squeamishness as he saw his friend shot down. He had wanted no part of this fight, none at all. But loyalty to a friend made the decision for him. Slowly, almost reluctantly, he went for his gun.

It was a poor decision.

When the shooting started, Chance had dropped the six-gun from his crippled fingers. He dived onto the ground and grabbed up the knife with his left hand. With an almost underhand, sweeping movement, he flung the knife at the man's belly. The knife sank in to the hilt, sounding like the piercing of a ripe melon.

His mouth tried to form words, ones that failed to pass through his trembling, parted lips. The bearded man struggled to wrench the knife from his gut and his eyes widened at the sight of his own blood.

As his strength faded and his knees buckled, he stared into the eyes of Chance McBride, the last sight his eyes would ever behold.

Chapter Five

Rising from the ground and wrenching the knife from the bearded one's dead body, he quickly sliced the Indian free. His body crashed into the dirt beneath him, bruised but still alive.

As the old warrior sat upon the ground, rubbing the rope burns on his neck, Amy rushed to her husband's side. "Are you all right, Chance?"

"I've never been better," he replied, "thanks to you."

Amy looked frightened, but relieved that he was unharmed. "I didn't have enough time to shoot the other one."

"Anybody who can shoot a rifle like that doesn't need a man around for protection."

"I wasn't sure that you'd come back with me, Chance, so I thought I needed to take some precautions. I taught myself to shoot. And besides, after finally getting you back, I wasn't about to let anybody take you away from me again."

Chance then walked over to where the Indian was sitting. He rose from the ground when I approached him. His face was dark and leathery from many days and hours in the sun and the wind. The years had traced their lines upon his rugged face and his shoulder-length hair was white as winter's first snowfall.

From the style of his moccasins and the clothes he was wearing, I could plainly see he was an Arapaho.

His eyes were dark as the midnight and they cut through a man, as if they were searching into one's very soul.

As Chance stared into those sober eyes, he was certain that they had seen many battles and that fear had been a stranger to them.

There was a fierce independence to this man, a quality that is certainly rare, yet common to his people. And he was courageous. Even when the noose was still around his neck, he had shown no fear of death.

His bravery earned Chance's admiration and he hoped to instill those same qualities in his own children, should he ever have any others.

"My name is Chance McBride," he said, while holding out his hand to the Indian. "Do you have a name?"

"I do not think you could say it. You can call me Yellow Bear."

He hesitated slightly before extending his hand. The Indian had a firm grip and his wiry arms still possessed the strength of a man half his age.

"McBride," said the Indian, as he pondered over the name. The name is spoken in our lodges. You give my people many cattle, when the little ones cried for food."

"Yes, that is true," he said. "But that was many years ago, when the weather was bad and the hunting parties couldn't travel."

"We have not forgotten," Yellow Bear said.

Amy had gone to get their horses and joined us there.

"This is Amy," Chance said.

"She is your woman?"

"Yes, she is."

Yellow Bear nodded. "It is good for a warrior to own a strong woman."

Amy flushed slightly.

"You're a long way from the reservation," Chance said.

"I am Yellow Bear of the Arapaho," he said. "The reservation is a home for squaws, not warriors. I leave."

"Men must be free," Chance said, "to hunt, to roam, to live, and to die."

"McBride speaks the truth."

Pointing at the two dead men, Chance asked, "Why do you figure they were trying to stretch your neck?"

"They say something about making a good Indian out of me."

Chance thought he detected a slight glint of humor in the old warrior's eyes and smiled at his response.

"The raven sent the men here."

"The raven?" Chance asked.

"Yes, the raven tried to help the wolf trap me."

"I don't have any idea what you're talking about."

"Sit down, McBride, and I will tell you."

Yellow Bear sat down cross-legged in front of a tree. And although Chance knew they should hurry to get away from this place, he and Amy sat down beside the Indian to listen to his story.

"When the long knives took my people to the reservation," Yellow Bear said, "at first I believed the Great Spirit wished me to be there. But after a couple of moons, I knew this was no place for a warrior, so I prayed to be free.

"For many nights, the wolf and the raven came and sat beside me while I talked to the Great Spirit. They listened, but could do nothing to help me. Brother Wolf said Yellow Bear could not walk away from the reservation on the ground. Raven said Yellow Bear couldn't fly high enough to leave."

"So, how did you get away from the reservation?" Chance said.

"I trust Brother Wolf," the Indian said. "He told me that I needed to become an eagle, which is powerful and flies much higher than the raven."

"So, you're saying Yellow Bear became an eagle to flee the reservation?"

"Yes, McBride. That is why you cannot say my name. I was given a new name when I became the eagle. It is sacred, so Whites are not permitted to speak it."

As Amy listened, she was enthralled by their conversation, which she believed was little more than legend and mythology. She wasn't sure how much of it she truly believed, but she feared to ask a question or to do anything that might interrupt them.

Yellow Bear stopped talking suddenly and stared at the woman for a moment.

"Why do you not believe the story of Yellow Bear?"

It was almost like the Indian read her thoughts the moment Amy was thinking them. She suddenly felt guilty and fearful, struggling to find the right words to say.

"I never said I didn't believe you."

"McBride's Woman will come to learn that Yellow Bear speaks the truth."

"Amy didn't mean to think anything ill of you," Chance said. "Please continue your story."

Yellow Bear sat silent for a time, like an old man trying to remember where he left off on a story. But before resuming, he briefly looked over at Amy and smiled. Then he said, "You will come to believe, woman of McBride.

"And when I became an eagle, the long knives had no power to keep me there. I flew high above their reach and left the reservation.

"But Raven was very angry, for he hates the eagle. The eagle flies much higher and closer to the Great Spirit than the Raven. It is for that reason, Raven wished to harm the eagle, so he became a trickster.

"Raven told Brother Wolf that he could help him feast on an eagle. Sometimes Brother Wolf can eat the raven, so catching them is no longer . . . How do you say it? Difficult? But the eagle? Brother Wolf can only dream of catching one, eating it, and gaining its power.

"That is why Raven brought me here, to the men with guns and ropes, and tricked these men so Brother Wolf could feast on the eagle. But Brother Wolf didn't know this eagle used to be his friend, Yellow Bear.

"Raven also didn't know that the Great Spirit, who is close to the eagle, would come to his aid and send McBride to help. I would thank you, but men with guns and ropes cannot harm an eagle. But Brother Wolf wishes to thank you."

"There is no need, Yellow Bear," Chance replied. "I was glad to help."

"Brother Wolf will not forget what you did," Yellow Bear said. "You kept him from being tricked by Raven and harming his friend. It is for that reason Brother Wolf will come to help you one day."

Yellow Bear climbed to his feet and said, "We should go now."

"You speak very good English," Chance said. "Where did you learn?"

When I was a child, a missionary came to our village. He taught us to read the White man's holy book."

The Indian studied Chance's face as if he was somewhat curious about him also. "Why did you not shoot the bearded one?" he said. "You had the gun in your hand and it is not the way of your people to fight their battles with knives."

"I cannot shoot a gun, Yellow Bear," he said, holding out his wounded right hand so the Indian could see it.

The old warrior studied the scar that Pete Ramsey's bullet inflicted there.

"This was done by the one they call Ramsey?" he asked.

Surprised by Yellow Bear's knowledge of the incident, Chance replied, "How did you know that?"

The Indian's face took on a stern look, seemingly annoyed by the question. "Before I became an eagle, I know of many things in the camps of the White man. It is how I stayed alive.

Chance couldn't argue with the reasoning of Yellow Bear, for he never stopped to consider the dilemma of the Arapaho. They were a people with few good choices, facing extinction at the coming of the Whites, or a life of restricted movement, confined and limited to the boundaries of a reservation.

"Now I am an eagle," Yellow Bear said, "and the eagle sees all."

With scarcely a wasted movement, the Indian helped to wrap their bodies in blankets and to lash them to each of their horses.

It was not a pleasant job, but it was a necessary chore. These men, no matter what they might have turned out to be, could still have families. And if there were any relatives, they would want their kinfolk to get a decent burial.

Yellow Bear, riding bareback, mounted his horse effortlessly.

A chill swept through Chance's soul as he thought about what might happen if anyone happened upon them there. With two dead white men and an Indian along, he would have a lot of explaining to do, if discovered.

Chance feared that strangers wouldn't even take the time to hear their story and would probably just try to kill them first. Anxious to be on their way, he swallowed hard, hoping they saw no one.

He held no grudges against the men they were forced to kill. Chance always believed that man is, above all, imperfect, and thereby capable of all manner of mischief.

The two bodies slung over their saddles were tough men, ones who followed a different path than the one Chance chose for himself. It had just been their misfortune that their two paths had been destined to cross.

As they mounted their horses, dawn was just starting to break above the Eastern treetops. They led the horses which carried the pair of bodies.

Chance had no idea if Yellow Bear would continue riding along with them, for an escaped, reservation Arapaho wasn't likely to be welcomed in Boot Hill Valley. A lot of men wouldn't trust an Indian, any Indian, but Chance had no fear of the aged warrior. Unlike the people of his own race, the Arapaho seldom forgot any act of kindness, no matter how small it might be.

And Yellow Bear knew that Chance's act of kindness wasn't a small one.

When they reached the edge of town, Chance and Amy continued onward while Yellow Bear remained behind.

"I will wait for you," he said.

Drawing rein in front of the undertaker's office, Chance dismounted and knocked on the door. A rustling of movement could be heard inside and the shade on the door was finally pushed aside.

"Don't you people know what time it is?" the man said, rubbing the sleep from his eyes. "What can I do for you?"

"We brought you some business."

"Okay! Okay!" he said. "Just give me a minute to pull on my shoes."

The undertaker, Douglas Watkins, had known Chance for years, but he failed to recognize him. A lack of sleep and last night's over-indulgence in a bottle of whiskey had affected both his sleep and his eyesight.

Grumbling and carrying a coal oil lamp, the undertaker shuffled out to the horses. The sun was coming up fully now, but it was still dark in the shadow of the buildings.

"It's a little early in the morning for gunplay," Watkins said.

He grabbed the bearded man's hair with his free hand, raising it until the lamp shone of the dead man's face. "This is Tom Quigley," Watkins said, letting the man's head fall. "He works for the Ramsey brothers."

Watkins lifted the other man's head and a look of panic marked the undertaker's face. "What happened to them?" he asked.

As Chance stared into the undertaker's eyes, he wondered at the terror he saw in them. "There was a little necktie social, just outside of town," he said, "and the guest of honor was an old, Arapaho warrior."

"An Arapaho? Aren't they on the reservation?"

"Not this one. Anyway, it seems that I interrupted their party and we had a disagreement over my lack of an invitation."

For the first time, the undertaker took note of the other rider. Watkins recognized her immediately, but wondered who this man was that accompanied her. Decent women seldom took early morning rides with men who weren't their husbands.

"Good morning," Mrs. McBride," Watkins said, his curiosity and suspicions running wild.

"Morning to you," Amy replied.

Amy McBride taking an early morning ride with a drifting cowhand, Watkins knew good gossip fodder when he found it. He was surprised to learn that Amy was actually that kind of woman, but Douglas still wondered how his opinion could have been so wrong about her. He couldn't wait to share this latest news with Sam Howard, down at the hardware store.

But just as the thoughts began to take root in his mind, he took another good look at the stranger's face. In the first dim lights of dawn, a man's face couldn't be seen too clearly. And although the voice had a strangely-familiar ring to it, Watkins still couldn't come up with a name. Then he stared at the stranger again.

"Chance McBride, is that you?" he asked, still unsure of himself.

"Yes, it is, Mr. Watkins."

"It's nice to see you and Amy back together again, marshal."

Chance nodded.

"I saw you yesterday, up on the hill at the other marshal's funeral," Watkins said. "A lot of good men have died, fallen from the gun of Pete Ramsey. It's a dirty shame," he added. "I hope nothing else happens to you."

"Why should it?"

"Because of the man with the scar," Watkins explained, his voice quivering slightly. "That was Bill Padgitt, Pete Ramsey's cousin."

"Pete's not going to like this one bit," Chance said.

"But that's not all."

"There's more?"

"Yes, there is, marshal. Do you recognize this horse?"

"No, should I?"

"I can't be absolutely certain, but I think this horse belonged to one of the raiders at the cemetery today."

As a result of the undertaker's remark, along with finally being able to see the horse for the first time in the ever-increasing light, Amy recognized it too.

"One of the riders was on a bay with a white splash on each leg," she said. "I'm absolutely positive this horse was ridden by one of the men who attacked us."

"So, that pretty well eliminates all doubt," Chance said, "about who was behind yesterday's attack on Boot Hill. No doubt Pete Ramsey was behind all of it."

The news came as a shock to Chance, considering that he couldn't effectively use a six-gun to defend himself. Now it was certain the Ramsey brothers would come gunning for him and he would be forced to fight them all.

But Chance's fears had nothing to do with his own safety; they had everything to do with Amy's.

Pete and his two brothers were brutal and vindictive men, ones who were certain to try and even up the score with him. Somehow, Chance knew he must regain the use of his right hand.

And soon.

Without speaking, Chance and Amy rode back to the edge of town. Each of them were fully aware of the dilemma they faced.

"I never should have come for you," Amy said. "If I'd simply left you alone, none of this would have ever happened."

"But you'd still be facing a threat from Pete. Please don't fret about me none, Amy. Both of them tried to kill me once, but they couldn't finish the job," he said with a smile. "And I don't die easy. You ought to know that by now. Next time I'll be ready for them."

"Not if you don't regain the use of your hand."

Their horses continued moving, nearing the edge of the town, within hearing distance of Yellow Bear. And as they approached, the old warrior listened in on their conversation.

"You can't even shoot a gun, Chance. What are you going to do?"

The two of them drew rein next to Yellow Bear.

"You saw me yesterday in Boot Hill. I can still shoot a rifle from my left shoulder."

"I still don't like it, Chance. I'm scared for you to face the Ramsey brothers with only one hand."

Before Chance could respond, Yellow Bear said, "McBride's hand, I can heal it."

Chance and Amy simply stared at the Indian, their mouths hanging open, unable to believe the words they just heard.

"What did you say?" Chance said.

The old Indian's visage had not changed, a solemn, almost expressionless stare that revealed little. "I can heal your hand," Yellow Bear said sternly.

"But Doc Arnold said that Chance wasn't likely to ever regain full use of it," Amy said, still skeptical of the Indian's bold declaration.

"Hold out your hand," Yellow Bear said.

Chance did as the Indian said and held out his hand.

The aged Indian took Chance by the wrist and studied the bullet scar like a tracker looks for signs upon the ground.

Yellow Bear nodded his head and frowned. "White man's medicine is not strong enough. I will heal the hand of McBride." Then he turned to Amy and said, "McBride came to help the eagle and he does not forget."

Even since Chance was a child, he had heard stories of strange Indian cures and remedies. He rarely paid them little mind, choosing rather to believe that they were no more than legends and fables.

But the wonders of science and medicine are never fully confined within the boundaries of today's version of accepted knowledge. Just because a person never learned of these ancient cures doesn't nullify their actual existence.

And since coming West, Chance had seen many of those old Indian remedies work, so he no longer discounted the powers of any of them.

He listened as Yellow Bear continued, "I cannot heal your hand now. I will return again when the moon is big in the sky."

"But how will you do it?" Amy said.

"I am a chief among my people. I, too, am a holy man."

"What does that mean?" she asked.

Chance leaned forward, crossing his arms on the horn of the saddle. Not waiting for Yellow Bear's answer, he said, "Amy, Yellow Bear is a medicine man, one who does magic or cures the sick. Some folks even believe they can read minds or predict future events."

"How is it you know so much about our ways, McBride?"

"I have heard much about them."

"You are wise to learn the ways of my people," Yellow Bear said, reining his horse around to leave. "The eagle must go now."

Chance offered his hand to Yellow Bear as a token of their trust for one another. The Arapaho accepted his gesture and galloped away.

Chance and Amy watched Yellow Bear ride towards the horizon, all at once disappearing from their vision. And despite spending several more minutes watching for him, the Indian never reappeared.

Although Chance and Amy thought it strange at the time, the two of them just assumed Yellow Bear had ridden into a low place on the trail, a place that simply obscured the Indian from their line of sight.

"Do you really think he'll come back, Chance?"

"Yes, I do, Amy, if nothing stops him from it."

Chapter Six

The news has a way of traveling quickly, particularly when that news is bad or tragic. Scandal and death are two occurrences which can seldom remain hidden for long, for their stories are often known to sprout wings, taking flight to anyone willing to lend an ear.

The vast territory of the West covers an extremely large area, but in reality, it's a remarkably small place. Newspapers are scarce in the sparsely-populated frontier and most of the news is carried by word of mouth.

The tiniest details of a gunfight spread like a raging wildfire in the West, from saloon to general store faster than gossip through a quilting bee. It was for that reason alone, the story of Bill Padgitt's death reached Pete Ramsey in only a matter of days.

Pete was not shocked upon learning about his cousin's death, for he already knew that it would surely happen one day. And although Pete was never a man known for his great caution, his cousin, Padgitt, was a fool, often taking needless risks in his desire for revenge.

Leaning back on his saddle next to the campfire, Pete held a scalding cup of black coffee and he stared off into the darkness. He tasted it slowly and swore at its bad taste.

"Can't you even make a decent pot of coffee?" he muttered to the cook, flinging it out towards the fire.

The cook mumbled something in response to Pete's complaint, but his comments were lost in the sounds of rattling pots and bawling cattle.

The other drovers relaxed around the friendly warmth of the campfire, as it glowed in the evening's cloak of darkness. In the distance, one could hear the soft strumming of a guitar, one of the hands trying to soothe the cattle.

Pete always knew that nothing good could come from his cousin's hatred of the Indians. And although Pete also killed several of them over the years, sometimes in defense of his own life, he held no lasting grudges against their people.

In Pete's mind, Bill Padgitt's shortcomings did absolutely nothing to excuse his death. Even though Pete didn't agree with his cousin, Padgitt was still kin. And the death of kinfolk always demanded retribution.

There was no other way; the death of his cousin must be avenged.

Duke Ramsey, who just finished taking his turn guarding the cattle interrupted Pete's thoughts. "Is it true?" he asked. "Did someone really kill our cousin?"

"Yes, Duke. It's true. You knew Bill. He always was a damned fool. Anybody with half a brain could've guessed his grudge for the Injuns would someday get him killed."

"Yep, I heard Bill talk about them too. What made him that way, Pete?"

"I figured you already knew the story."

"No, it happened before I was even born.

"I know that, Duke, but I always figured he told you about it."

"No. No, he never did."

Pete got up from his seat, walked over to the fire, and poured himself and Duke another couple cups of bad coffee. When he returned, he handed one to Duke, tasted a sip of his own and scowled.

"When Bill was a child," Pete said, "a raiding, Injun party attacked our uncle's ranch. It was a total massacre, with no mercy whatsoever for the victims. The house was set ablaze and Bill's mother and father, our aunt and uncle, were killed, leaving him an orphan.

"Our folks came along only a couple of hours after the raid. I think Ma was all swelled up with you at the time. Pa told me that he just couldn't believe the gruesome sight that was laid out right there before them.

"The ranch house our uncle lived in was nearly big as Texas, but all that remained was just the smoke and ashes. Scattered around the burned out ranch house were the naked and dismembered bodies of our family."

"I never heard any of this," Duke said.

"Eldon, Bill's father, was found laying just outside the house's front door, "Pete said. "He had been inside the house and rushed outside at the first sign of the attack. His busted rifle lay on the ground beside him, not too far from his hand.

"There were heavy signs of blood around what was left of him, showing that he likely took a number of others with him. It was clear to everyone, the man died game. Bill's mom, Pa didn't even want to talk about her," Pete continued. "All he'd ever say was that they left her naked and violated. I never asked him anything more."

Duke drank the last of his coffee and moved over to squat next to the fire. "I have to ask. Who killed him, Pete?"

"It was McBride . . ." Pete replied. He hesitated, as his words had their desired effect. ". . . and his woman."

Duke stared into the eyes of his brother. "We should have killed that marshal."

"We will, Duke. We will."

* * *

An owl hooted outside Chance's window and he rose from the bed, unable to sleep. All through the night, he hadn't been able to get the recent funerals out of his mind.

Several good marshals had been murdered and their deaths continued to haunt him. Chance couldn't seem to rise above the guilt and the
feeling that he was largely responsible for all that took place.

If I had done my job, he thought, *none of those men would have had
to die.*

Remembering the shooting while he stared at his scarred hand,
Chance longed for even a small taste of whiskey.

Chance was now faced with two battles that he must fight.

It was certain that Pete Ramsey and his brothers would long for
revenge for the killing of his cousin and Chance's terrible craving for
the bottle wasn't going away without a fight either.

Yellow Bear claimed that he could heal Chance's hand and he desperately wanted to believe that the Indian could really do it. But as
much as he desired it, Chance wasn't about to start counting on a miracle.

Chance knew he must plan on defeating them with the skills that he
already possessed. And to do that, he knew his mind couldn't be in any
way clouded by the bottle. Protecting Amy, and staying alive to do it,
would take every bit of savvy he could muster.

And a whole lot of luck to go with it.

As soon as the Ramsey brothers finished driving their cattle to the
railhead, Chance knew they would come for him. Not only was his own
life at risk, but Amy's was on the line as well.

This time, Chance had no intention of letting her down again.

He rose from the bed, pulled on his pants and his boots quietly, and
tried not to disturb Amy. Although he'd been living there again for the
past few weeks, Chance still fumbled his way through the darkness in
a house from which he was absent for nearly three years. Finally, he
located the coal oil lamp.

He struck a match, lifted the globe, and lit the end of the wick. As the flame caught, it filled the room with its illumination. Putting on his hat and grabbing his Winchester, he eased the door open and went outside.

The air was still warm and a gentle breeze tugged at his sleeves. It was a bright evening outside and the lamp was scarcely needed. He only left the lamp lit because he knew it would certainly still be dark inside the barn.

Upon reaching the barn, he hung the lamp on a peg above the door. The horses immediately sensed his presence and began to nicker softly.

Gently he spoke to them, "How are you doing this morning?"

They blew through their nostrils, seemingly in return to Chance's greeting.

As Chance looked around the barn, he still marveled to see the amount of hay inside and how the building was now in such good repair. He knew that Amy wasn't capable of doing all of this on her own, so it was obvious that a fair number of the townspeople had generously given of their own time and resources to help her.

And for their many kindnesses to Amy, Chance felt he owed the people of Boot Hill Valley a great debt, something which might only be fully paid by somehow keeping them safe.

Leaning his rifle against the edge of their stall, Chance grabbed a nearby pitchfork and forked some hay in front of the horses. The animals didn't waste any time in going after the forage.

While the horses contentedly fed on the hay, Chance thought about his life and the twisted path it had taken. At one time, everything in life seemed to be going his way. But it only took a few circumstances to change all that.

He and Amy were back together now, but their life hadn't exactly turned into one of those fairy tales that he once read. Instead, it was more like a nightmare, the two of them unable to escape the evil shadow of the Ramsey brothers.

The horses needed some water, so he headed for the well, bucket in hand. He drew the first pail, took a drink, and splashed some of the cool, clear water on his face. Despite his desire for a drink of something stronger, Chance felt it was mighty good to be home, enjoying the taste of water from his own well.

As he sat there next to the well, the wind carried the faint smell of bacon. Chance smiled. *Amy must now be stirring*, he thought, *fixing me some breakfast*. Once again, he was truly glad to be home.

Returning to the barn, the horses were waiting for a drink and greedily slurped up the water Chance gave them. He made two more trips to the well before the animals' thirst was satisfied.

Just as Chance was getting ready to return to the house, his attention was captured by some kind of movement outside the barn. Rushing over to douse the light, he waited, the minutes passing like hours.

When facing danger, Chance believed the first one to move is often the first one to die. But as he waited, he wished that Amy wasn't in the house alone.

The possibility of danger will often cause the mind to play tricks on a man, causing him to conjure up all manners of evil.

Maybe the Ramsey brothers had returned, looking to settle the score.

But as fast as the thought came to his mind, Chance discounted it. And he knew a trail drive cannot be accomplished in only a few brief weeks.

Just as Chance decided that the sound was nothing to fear and he started to return to the house, he heard it again.

Although it didn't sound exactly like boot steps, this time the noise had been louder, like the sound of something moving slowly across the ground, moving closer.

Waiting inside one of the horse stalls, Chance quietly eared back the hammer of his rifle, pointing the gun towards the door.

Although he had done relatively little shooting with the gun on his opposite shoulder, Chance knew it was unlikely that he would miss from that short a distance.

From there, he waited . . .

The sound seemed to be coming closer, moving slowly, warily. And then the door slammed open and a lone figure loomed in the doorway, silhouetted by the moonlight behind him.

"Hold it right there," Chance said, revealing his position, but not yet exposing himself to the threat of gunfire. "What do you want?"

"The time has come," he said. "I am here for McBride."

It was Yellow Bear.

Chapter Seven

As time passed, Chance often forgot about Yellow Bear's promise to return when the moon was full.

And although he'd been anxiously expecting the Indian's return, the prospect of his return didn't dominate Chance's daily thoughts. Now he was frightened.

Until the Indian returned, Chance could always live with the prospect of his hand being healed. However, if Yellow Bear's treatment failed to work, then his hope would be gone, leaving him nothing else upon which he might now place his trust.

And then Chance must fully face his grim future, once again knowing he would only have the use of one good hand.

At the sound of the Indian's familiar voice, he lowered his rifle.

"Howdy, Yellow Bear," he said, moving out of the shadows. "It's good to see you again."

"McBride, I see you are not dead yet."

In spite of himsself, Chance laughed at his comment. "No, but the day's still early."

For the first time, Chance noticed the bag the Indian was carrying.

Yellow Bear seemed to read his thoughts and lifted the bag in his hand. "This is strong medicine. It will chase away the evil spirits that now trouble you."

"Chance," Amy's voice called out from the house, "your breakfast is ready."

Chance grabbed the lantern and headed for the house. Yellow Bear followed him, still carrying the bag he brought.

The Indian merely stared while Chance stopped to wash his hands in a bowl outside the house and then dried them on a towel that hung there. Then he followed Chance inside the house.

"We have a guest," Chance said upon his entrance.

"I'm pleased to have you, Yellow Bear. Welcome to my home," Amy said. "May I get you something to eat?"

The old Indian nodded, refusing to turn down the hospitality of a friend.

Chance was not surprised that Yellow Bear chose to eat with them.

If Chance had been a guest in their Arapaho village, it would have offended the Indian hosts if he turned down their kindness, so it was certain that Yellow Bear wouldn't refuse to eat and risk insulting them as well.

They sat down at the kitchen table, filling their plates with bacon and fried potatoes. Meanwhile, Amy continued working in the kitchen slicing more strips from the slab of bacon. She smiled as she watched them, a woman taking pleasure in the feeding of hungry men.

Yellow Bear ate several servings of potatoes and nearly a pound of bacon and Chance finished off a substantial portion himself. They also drank over two pots of coffee.

From the old warrior's lean and wiry frame, it was hard for Chance to imagine how the man could eat so much. He was also surprised because the Indians were known for their rare ability to often survive with meager amounts of food and water.

After breakfast was finished, Amy cleared the table and Yellow Bear prepared to work on Chance's hand.

The aged Indian stood to his feet and removed something from his bag. Then he began to shake this powdery substance all around the room, all the while he was chanting something in his native tongue.

Although Chance couldn't fully speak their language, the Indian's tongue wasn't completely unfamiliar to him. Occasionally, he could pick out some words and phrases the old warrior was speaking, which told him the ceremony was supposed to drive away any bad spirits that might dwell in the room.

When that part of the ritual was completed, Yellow Bear pulled out his knife, an ugly, bone-handled one with a eight-inch blade. He placed the blade of it in the fire for a few minutes, until the blade was bright red.

Amy had been watching closely, trying to remain brave, but the fear in her eyes revealed her true feelings. She winced as she saw the Indian draw the hot steel from the fireplace.

With a smile and a friendly wink, Chance tried in vain to reassure Amy that everything was all right. But when Yellow Bear pulled the knife from the fire, the doubts also came to Chance's mind as well.

Both of them were more-than-familiar with dozens of hair-raising stories of what some renegade Indians did with a knife. Since childhood, they had each heard many stories of Indian uprisings and bloodshed, tales which now flooded back into their minds, causing them to think only of the worst.

A trace of a smile came across the Indian's face and his dark eyes twinkled as he once again seemed to read their minds.

"You are both safe," he said, scarcely hiding his amusement. "I haven't scalped any Whites for many moons. Now give me your hand."

Yellow Bear lifted his hot knife and studied the nasty scar on Chance's right hand. The old warrior turned the hand over slowly, looking at both sides of the wound.

He then placed the hot, knife blade against the palm of his hand, drawing some of his own blood.

"The knife is sharp," he said, with no apparent recognition of pain.

Chance nodded, wondering what the Indian would do next.

The Indian didn't keep him in suspense for too long before he began cutting a small, cross-shaped incision across the old bullet hole. Chance winced from the pain, but managed to remain silent.

For several moments, Yellow Bear allowed the new wound to bleed freely. He then returned the knife to his sheath, took Chance's hand, and spoke some other words which were unknown to them.

Then he joined their palms in a handshake, allowing their blood to intermingle between the two, fresh wounds, not unlike a blood-brother ceremony.

"You now have blood of the Arapaho, which should make you stronger."

"And you have the blood of the Whites," Chance added.

"Not enough to harm me," Yellow Bear said with a smile.

Next, the Indian removed a pouch from his bag and poured a foul-smelling liquid into Chance's open wound. At first the liquid burned like fire and then the pain subsided, until it was completely gone.

Amy continued to watch closely, unwilling to leave the room or the man she loved. Beyond her doubts, she realized that Chance must regain the use of his hand in order to defend himself against Ramsey.

Every last ounce of faith resting in her soul made her want to believe that Yellow Bear could help. But she also grappled with the fear of getting her hopes too high, only to be disappointed later.

Looking up from his work, the Indian looked at the woman and momentarily smiled at her. Then he returned to his business as before.

If Doc Arnold had been unable to do anything for her husband, Amy felt that it was quite unlikely that an old Indian's strange rituals could change anything in Chance's condition.

But deep within Amy's heart, a faint, glimmering light of hope remained.

Yellow Bear told Chance to work the hand, so he flexed his hand into a clenched fist. It felt no stronger or more capable than before and Chance, who'd been expecting an instant miracle, was somewhat disheartened by the fact.

The hand felt every bit as stiff as before, but he continued to work with it, until the Indian told him to stop.

He then carefully applied an unfamiliar herbal poultice to the fresh, knife wound and tied it on there with Chance's bandana.

Yellow Bear sat back in the chair, his work complete.

"You must wait now. Do nothing with your hand tonight," Yellow Bear explained, as he went to the door. "I will return tomorrow."

The Indian left the room without any further comment, leaving Chance staring at his bandaged hand.

Chance looked down at his damaged hand and wondered if he would ever be able to use a six-gun again.

Yellow Bear had a way about him that made Chance want to trust him. The Indian said his hand could be healed and something about the old Arapaho made the former marshal believe his promise.

A gentle hand touched his arm and he turned to look into a pair of lovely, but worried eyes. His mind searched for the proper words, anything to relieve her fears.

"It will be all right, Amy," he said, knowing that his uncertain words of comfort might not ring true. "I'm sure of it."

The two of them had done everything that could be done, and now they must wait. Yellow Bear said he would return tomorrow.

The day passed slowly.

* * *

The town of Boot Hill Valley was gripped in fear and uncertainty, caused by the death of Bill Padgitt.

Fear.

This malady was no stranger to its citizens, for fear had become rather commonplace there, common as the sounds of children playing or the blistering heat of the afternoon sun.

There were few secrets inside Boot Hill Valley. Everyone in the community knew that Bill was a cousin to the Ramsey brothers, raised as one of their own. The locals also knew all too well what Pete's reaction would be, holding the entire town responsible for Bill's death.

The clock continued to tick, the minutes and hours passing swiftly, bringing closer the end of Pete's yearly trail drive. Then it was certain he would return to pillage the town, his heart set on revenge.

Nobody was left to stand in Pete's way, to hold forth the banner of law and order; nobody was strong enough to defeat him. Several marshals had tried valiantly, but their attempts all ended in the same manner . . .

In utter failure and death.

With the death of Bill Padgitt, McBride brought Pete's anger upon the town, but few of the townspeople blamed Chance for it.

Of course, there were also more than a few mutterings about whether saving the life of one, aged Indian was worth the trouble it would bring upon them. At the same time, many of them also knew that Chance would have risked his life for them as well, in much the same way he did at the cemetery.

If anything was to be done about the Ramsey brothers, the people would have to do it themselves.

Another marshal couldn't be found.

At this point, the citizens would have gladly aided McBride, or any other uncrippled lawman, but they had neither the courage nor the desire to fight by themselves. These were not bad people, just frightened ones.

Not one citizen of Boot Hill Valley expected a one-handed, former marshal to defend their town. And most of them thought McBride had already sacrificed enough, giving up the use of his hand in performance of his regular duties. They also realized that Chance already had too many problems of his own, with his drinking and Pete's lust for revenge.

Each of them remembered when Pete came to the town meeting, threatening to take whatever he wanted. They knew he usually did what he promised, ever-confident on the backing of his two brothers. It was certain that when Pete returned to town, bent on revenge, no one would be safe from the man . . .

Women, children . . . nobody.

The town leaders, realizing the immediate threat to the town, contacted several current or former lawmen around the territory, hoping one of them would accept the job of marshal. Unfortunately, Boot Hill Valley's bloody reputation preceded their queries and there were no takers.

Of course, none of the local citizens wanted the job. There was no one capable or willing in the town, someone who could adequately hope to stand up to the Ramsey brothers.

The town needed someone to champion its cause, a man who had enough steel in his backbone to face the brothers on their own terms. The man must also be a gunfighter, for it was certain that gunplay would be inevitable in ultimately stopping them.

The Ramsey brothers were cold-blooded killers, evil men who would stop at nothing. In order to deal with them, a man would have to possess extraordinary courage and a willingness to boldly confront violence. The brothers understood nothing else. In addition, the man must also be blessed with a great measure of wisdom, so that he might determine when such force would be necessary.

Doc Arnold knew all these things and he only knew one man who was up to the job . . .

Chance McBride.

As the doctor's black surrey bounced along the twisted, bumpy road, on its way back to town, he wondered what he would say to them when he arrived.

Doc Arnold knew this was a fool's errand. Chance could do nothing for the town. But still, some unexplained, inner voice compelled him to go see the former marshal.

He hated to intrude on the young couple, especially since they only recently were reunited, but it could not be helped. Some inner urging pushed Arnold onward and he already learned it wise to obey his first instincts.

Arnold had just finished treating an injured cowhand, on a small ranch, five miles outside of town. The cowpoke had been thrown from his horse, caught his foot in the stirrup, and was dragged for several feet before another cowhand rushed to his aid. The man was lucky to be alive.

As the surrey rounded the final bend, the once-peaceful, little town loomed before him. The doctor drew rein outside Chance's house. Reaching underneath the seat of his surrey, he retrieved a carrot he placed there earlier that evening, and stepped down.

Arnold patted his faithful horse on the neck, feeding him the carrot as he did so. "You're a good old fellow," he said. "I'll be back soon."

It was still early evening and a pleasant breeze tugged at the doctor's coat sleeves. And although the sun had already fallen, the moon's full brightness lighted his way.

Chance was sitting at the table, cleaning and reloading a six-gun that he still didn't have the capacity to use when the doctor's knock sounded on the door. The knock surprised him, for he wasn't expecting any visitors at this time of the evening.

"Anyone coming to see you?" he said to Amy.

Amy shook her head.

Cocking the gun with his good hand and praying he wouldn't need it, Chance opened the door to the smiling face of Doc Arnold.

"Howdy, Doc," he said, glad to see a friendly face, one that didn't still look on him with pity. "Come on in"

"I'd be glad to," the doctor said, "just as soon as you get that muzzle pointed away from my chest."

"Sorry, Doc," Chance said, lowering the gun and releasing the hammer. "A man can never be too careful."

Amy had been busy when the doctor arrived, rustling about in the kitchen. Although his mind had been elsewhere and he was paying little attention to her activities, Chance now noticed the delightful smell of fresh-baked, apple pie which was filling the room.

"How are you doing, my dear?" the doc said, removing his hat.

"Much better, now," she said, casting a glance in her husband's direction.

The physician's knowing glance indicated that he understood the reason for Amy's good spirits and he, too, was pleased by Chance's return.

Amy walked over and took the doctor's hat. "May I get you a cup of coffee and a piece of apple pie?" she said. "I just made it."

"Sure, dear. Thank you. That's an invitation I've been fervently praying for since I first walked up on your porch."

Chance and the doctor each took a place at the table. For just a moment, Arnold briefly glanced at the gun which Chance placed on the end of the table, but he said nothing more about it.

The two men traded mindless observations on the weather until Amy returned with the two pieces of pie and two cups of steaming, black coffee.

"If you'll excuse me," Amy said, "I'll let you two gentlemen have some privacy to talk."

The doctor nodded and thanked her before she returned to other duties in the kitchen.

Chance was the first to break the awkward silence.

"I've got a sneaking suspicion that this isn't just a social call. What can I do for you, Doc?"

"I'm not sure you can do anything," he shrugged, taking a long, deep sip of his coffee. "I've never been very good at beating around the bush, so I'll come right to the point, son. The Valley needs your help."

Chance said nothing as he drank his coffee, seemingly uninterested.

The doctor continued his plea, disturbed by the former marshal's silence. "The Ramsey brothers will be returning from their trail drive soon. And if you remember hearing about the promise Pete made at the town meeting, you already know what kind of danger we're in."

The doctor paused, taking another taste of his pie and chasing it down with some more coffee. "Worst of all," he added, hoping to win the young man over, "the womenfolk will be in serious danger."

"What can I do?"

The doctor didn't hesitate. "We need you back. As marshal."

The doctor's reply came as a shock to him. "What's the matter? Can't get anyone better to take the job?" he said, a little ashamed for his harsh tone of voice.

Arnold did not hesitate in his answer, responding with a refreshing sense of honesty that Chance could only pause to admire.

"No, they can't, son. There is nobody else."

"Well, I'm grateful that you leveled with me, Doc."

Theirs was a meager house, with small rooms and a shortage of space. And through no fault of her own, while still busy in the kitchen, Amy had overheard portions of their conversation.

Chance had said nothing to the doctor about Yellow Bear and had somehow managed to hide the fresh bandage on his hand from the doctor.

Although she decided to follow Chance's lead and remain silent, Amy was strangely baffled as to her husband's reason for his silence and concealment regarding his hand. She just couldn't think of any good reason to keep that information from the doctor.

"Listen, Chance. The townspeople can defeat Pete and his brothers themselves," Arnold said, "but first they need a spark, someone to rally behind. And I truly believe you're the man they need."

"But this is my fight, Doc. I'm the one who killed Padgitt. The town had nothing to do with it, so I should be the one who pays the fiddler. Not them."

Amy returned from the other room, to pour them some more coffee and to pick up their empty plates. "More pie?" she asked softly.

"No, thank you," Doc said, followed by the same response from Chance.

Amy smiled and returned to the kitchen.

"Maybe it is your fight," the doctor said, "but do you really think Pete Ramsey is smart enough to draw that kind of distinction. He will hold the Valley responsible for Padgitt's death, not just you."

The kindly, town doctor made a compelling argument for which Chance had no good answer.

"Why me?" he said, puzzled by the sudden interest in a drunken and crippled, former marshal. "You know I'm nothing more than a miserable drunkard, with only one good hand."

"Pete Ramsey wants you dead, Chance. Sooner or later, he'll come back here, looking for you. If you held the Valley, we can join hands, so to speak, and defeat him together.

"I know you, son. Nothing, not even a handicap can stop you, if you set your mind to it." The doctor looked Chance straight in the eyes, his gaunt features peering into the very depth of the young man's soul. "You're a proud man, Chance McBride. You're no drunkard. If you were still on the bottle, you wouldn't still be here with Amy."

Doc Arnold was much more than a seasoned veteran when it came down to the art of persuasion and Chance was beginning to run low on excuses.

Reluctantly, Chance had to admit that his arguments touched some hidden chord, deep within himself. Arnold's words rekindled a spark, a genuine sense of duty that the former marshal just couldn't shirk. He smiled at the old man's craftiness and insight into the minds and hearts of others around him.

"Does anyone know what you're here to see me about, or are you authorized to speak for the mayor now, doc?"

He smiled, slyly.

"Like you said yourself, no one else will take the job. The mayor will ultimately pin a badge on the chest of anyone fool enough to accept it. Well," the doctor said, "are you fool enough?"

"Please let me sleep on it tonight, you old meddler," Chance said. "I'll give you an answer tomorrow."

"Never put off until tomorrow those things which should be done today, son."

"Don't push your luck, Doc," he warned, jokingly. "Now get out."

Arnold nodded and headed for the door. "I'd better go, before I wear out my welcome."

Amy returned from the other room. She waited by the door, smiling sweetly, as she handed the doctor his hat. "Good evening, doctor," she said, closing the door behind him.

As Amy turned to face him, Chance could see the bewilderment in her glance. "Why didn't you tell him about your hand?"

Chance took another sip of coffee, which had now gotten cold. He scowled at the taste of it. "I didn't want to get anyone's hopes up, least of all, mine. And if the hand doesn't heal, it will make no difference anyway."

She nodded in agreement.

"Let's turn in," Amy suggested. "It's been a long day."

Amy was right. The day had been a long one.

"You won't have to ask me twice. I'm plumb worn out," he said. "Just give me a couple of minutes and I'll join you."

The pistol rested on the table and Chance stared at it for several minutes. He knew it was his only hope against the Ramsey brothers. If Yellow Bear failed, how could he protect Amy? How could he defend the town? How?

More than ever, he wondered what the future would hold.

Chapter Eight

True to his word, just as Chance expected, Yellow Bear returned the following day at sunup.

The first knife-like beams of sunlight sliced their way through the kitchen window pane. Their early arrival did not find Chance sleeping. Instead, he'd been awake for hours, pacing back and forth, anxiously awaiting the dawn.

In a land made for dreamers, Chance saw only nightmares.

Once more, he spent another restless night, tossing and turning, memorizing every speck or flaw on the bedroom ceiling. Sleep had become a fleeing, mounted desperado, constantly being pursued, but generally eluding his capture.

In the earliest, piercing light of sunrise, the slightest smudge would be clearly seen on the windows. None could be found. Chance knew a lot of elbow grease had been applied in their house. Amy's routine labors were not hidden from even the most casual observer.

The oaken, hardwood floors were well-polished, with nary a hint of dust or cobwebs everywhere. The indications of a caring woman's touch were all around them.

Amy took great pride in the cleanliness of her house. As further evidence of her devotion to duty, an old broom rested in the corner, falling apart from many, endless hours of employment. Amy's mop was equally abused.

When Chance was drinking, cleanliness had not been important to him. He'd been content to live anywhere, in any kind of a mess, just so long as he had a bottle. But now that he'd given up the whiskey, he was once again growing appreciative of a woman's touch.

Chance stared at his bandaged, right hand, wondering if he would ever shoot with it again. But his thoughts were broken by a sound outside his door. He grabbed his rifle from above the mantle, jacked a shell in the chamber, and pointed it at the door with his left hand.

"Come on in, if you're friendly," Chance said, bringing his gun into alignment, just about belt level. "If you ain't friendly, come in shootin'."

The door began to open slowly, almost hesitantly. His finger tensed on the trigger in preparation for the worst.

A dark, nearly brownish, weathered face greeted him. The man's stern, expressionless features broke into a smile, from only one side of his mouth.

It was Yellow Bear.

The aged Indian spoke slowly, deliberately, surprising Chance with his extraordinary grasp of his language.

"If this is how you welcome a friend," Yellow Bear said, "I not want to be your enemy."

Chance lowered his rifle.

"Come on in, Yellow Bear."

After entering the house, the Indian warrior wasted no time and said nothing more as he began his mysterious healing ritual. The entire ceremony lasted for several minutes, as Yellow Bear began chanting something in his native tongue.

Amy was awakened by the sound of an unfamiliar voice and came out from her room to investigate. She immediately walked up alongside her husband, curiously watching this strange, Indian rite.

"Do you really think he can heal your hand, Chance?" she whispered.

"I don't know, Amy, but we shouldn't be too long in finding out."

Yellow Bear pointed at my hand, saying nothing, wanting me to hold it out to him. He removed an eagle's feather from his garments and moved it above the bandaged hand.

Speechless and carefully watching all that was taking place inside her small house, Amy stood beside him.

Next, he carefully unwrapped the bandana from the wounded hand. The herbal poultice, which was now stained blood-red, fell to the floor.

Amy gasped suddenly, startled by the unbelievable sight that was now before them . . .

* * *

The long line of cattle continued to move onward, like a strand of cord stretched out along the vast expanse of prairie. The year had been one of the driest ever and a huge cloud of dust was raised by the herd's procession.

Suddenly shattering the usual silence of the frontier were the sounds of bawling cattle and the occasional shouts or shrill whistles of the drovers. A chuck wagon rattled along beside them and the pots and kettles clanked against each other in the back.

The cattle's passing did not go without notice. A couple dozen curious prairie dogs stood on their hind legs, carefully studying the procession of men and cattle. Realizing that the trespassers would do them no harm, the prairie dogs went back to their contented activities.

Jason Ramsey had been riding drag since sunup. He had eaten trail dust the entire day, with his bandana doing little to filter it away from his mouth and nose. From time to time, he could be heard cursing the beeves, since Jason had no real interest in the hard work involved in conducting a trail drive.

Yet Jason always enjoyed the prestige and attention that went along with owning thousands of cattle and living on a huge ranch. Perhaps most of all, he enjoyed the attention of the ladies when he bragged about the number of cattle and acres they controlled.

He was a young man, full of dash and swagger, always confident in his own sense of power and the inability of others to rarely challenge them.

Jason's hat was pulled down low over his eyes and he squinted against the ever-growing cloud of dust and the brutal onslaught of the noonday sun. His shirt reeked from the pungent mixture of trail dust and sweat. Jason removed his hat, wiping his forehead on his sleeve. He longed for a nice, hot bath, a shot of whiskey, and the willing company of a woman, but not necessarily in that particular order.

A lone rider, from the front of the herd, came riding his way. Jason strained his eyes, trying to recognize the cowboy's face. It was Isaac Cox, one of his brother's newer hands.

Jason pulled the neckerchief from off his nose and mouth, happy to be relieved from his place on drag. "It's about time," he grumbled, slapping the spurs to his mount.

Cox shouted after him, "The boss is wanting to see you."

Jason continued riding, throwing up his hand in acknowledgement of the message.

While jawing and sharing some friendly banter with the cook, Pete Ramsey rode alongside the chuck wagon. His horse trotted along leisurely, matching the pace of the wagon's team and occasionally switching its tail at a bothersome fly landing on the roan's haunches.

"Doggone it, Pete," the cook grumbled, angered by a drover's comment about the food, "my grub ain't so bad." He spat a green stream of tobacco juice on the ground next to the wagon.

"Iffen they don't like my cooking, let them go somewhere else. It's a hundred miles in any direction to the nearest hash house," he continued. "They might want to keep that in mind."

Pete was busy ignoring the cook's everyday bellyaching, his mind already preoccupied with the rolling of another cigarette. He shoved the smoke between his lips, looked at the cook and smiled. Then he struck a match, lit the cigarette, and casually enjoyed a couple of deep puffs.

"Listen, Slim," Pete replied, trying to sooth the cook's anger, "I'm sure the boys meant nothing by it."

Slim, not willing to accept Pete's explanation, blurted out, "I'm not going to take any more of it." Maybe I'll just give them all some biscuits laced with Castor Oil."

The trail drive had been a dry, brutal one, the days long and the nights short, leaving men's tempers already at the breaking point. Ramsey reined his horse around, his teeth clenched, coldly staring into the eyes of his cook.

"I'm not going to take any more of you, Slim," Pete said. "You've done nothing but gripe since this drive started and I'm just about fed up with it.

"I've got two thousand head of skittish cow-critters to get to the rail head and not much time to get them there. The last thing I need is to be a nursemaid for a whiny, trail cook," Pete added. Do you understand me?"

Red-faced, Ramsey flicked away the freshly-rolled cigarette to the ground and his hand tensed over the butt of his gun. "If you cause me anymore grief, Slim, or I even begin to suspect I got the scours from a dose of Castor Oil, I'll . . ."

Pete's threat fell on deaf ears, the words muffled and forgotten in the sounds of approaching hoof beats.

Fully aware of Pete's instant capacity for violence, the cook breathed a sigh of relief, glad for the sudden interruption.

"Isaac said you wanted to see me, Pete," Jason said.

"Yea, that's right. I've got a little job for you."

"What is it?"

Pete neglected to answer the question until he built another smoke. "I want you to ride back to town and keep an eye on things." He lit the cigarette and took a long, deep puff. "If McBride or his wife make any move to leave town, I want to know where they go.

"McBride killed Padgitt and I want to make damn sure he pays for it, along with the rest of the town. Running won't do him no good."

Jason nodded.

"This time around," Pete said, "I'll shoot a lot more than just his hand." Pete laughed out loud, his eyes taking on a crazed appearance. "Then I'll have that handsome McBride woman all to myself."

"You can count on me," Jason replied, reining his horse around to go.

"And Jason," Pete said, causing Jason to draw rein and turn his mount to face him.

"What's that?"

"Just make sure you don't do anything until Duke and I get there. Just watch," Pete added. "That town needs to be taught a lesson and we'll all do it together."

"You bet," Jason said, waving as he rode away.

For the next several minutes, Pete sat there on horseback, enjoying his smoke and watching the horse and rider disappear over the horizon.

Despite his explicit instructions, Pete was completely unaware of the plans that were now already being formulated in his brother's mind.

Jason wondered why Pete and Duke should have all the fun. After all, Chance McBride only had one good hand. And that one wasn't his gun hand.

He pondered over the notion, the prospects of his own success growing with every hoof fall.

"I'll just kill him myself," Jason said, speaking to his horse. "Pete and Duke will have to treat me like a man then."

It's been a long time since I've set foot inside a saloon, he thought. *That will be the first stop, then McBride.*

The longer he road, the better the idea sounded to him.

A one-handed marshal, he thought.

"It will be easy," Jason said out loud. "It will be easy."

A smile came across his face.

Chapter Nine

Thinking that their eyesight might be playing tricks on them, Chance and Amy continued to stare at his hand in slack-jawed disbelief. The ominous silence was only broken by a rooster's crow.

"Do you see that, Chance?"

"Yep," Chance said, turning his hand one way and then the other. "But I still don't believe it."

Amy smiled and replied, "It's . . . it's a miracle."

Only the day before, Yellow Bear sliced the palm of Chance's hand with his skinning knife, leaving a fresh, deep wound. The old Arapaho's blade made a clean cut, but nevertheless, a deep one.

But the cut was now gone, without any trace that it was ever there.

There should have been a fresh wound on his palm, a mark or bloody stripe, something, anything to indicate the skin had only recently been cut.

But it had all vanished.

All that remained of the old Indian's remedy was the blood-stained, herbal poultice.

Nothing else.

Chance worked his hand, first flexing the fingers, then closing them. Only some minor pain and stiffness remained, but it was soon forgotten, little more than a simple inconvenience.

Chance raced into the bedroom to locate his six-gun.

Amy did not follow him.

She knew this was something a man must do alone.

As he saw the gun just sitting there on his nightstand, he remembered the attack and what it had nearly cost him. And for the first time in days, Chance lusted for a taste of whiskey.

Fighting the doubt inside of him, Chance picked up the gunbelt and buckled it around his hips. His hands trembled slightly as he tied the rawhide lacing around his leg.

He stared at the scar on the back of his hand and recalled the number of good men who died trying to protect Boot Hill Valley. Hatred and bitterness filled his soul.

It is now or never, he thought. *The hand must be tested.*

Chance had to know.

He feared to try.

Gently, hesitantly removing the gun from its holster, he discovered that he could now ear back the hammer and work the trigger, perhaps better than he did before.

The next time, he palmed the gun a little quicker, earing back the hammer as he drew and the gun came level. It was a skill he thought was gone forever.

He stared at the gun in the palm of his hand, bewildered that the pain and stiffness was all but completely gone. Then he reholstered it.

Finally, Chance slapped leather and felt the gun spring into his hand with a speed and ease he had never known before. He repeated it again and again, each draw becoming swifter, easier, and more fluid.

The wound was gone. The stiffness was gone. And nothing else mattered.

As quickly as it came, the insane craving for liquor left him.

Except for one visible reminder, the scar on the back of Chance's hand, the Ramseys' attack on him would have suddenly become little more than an unpleasant memory. Perhaps it would always be there, reminding Chance of the danger of being careless, a warning of being too slow.

The scar also served as a grim reminder, underlining the necessity to defeat the Ramsey brothers.

And the next time they met, Chance knew he would be ready.

Amy waited for him as he came out of the bedroom. Fear and doubt filled her eyes, as she awaited a nod, a smile, anything to indicate that his hand was now all right.

Chance's eyes were expressionless as he faced her.

With tears showing in her eyes, Amy studied his face, wanting to ask the question, but also fearing what the answer might be.

As a big smile came to Chance's face, Amy wondered no more, running over and leaping into his arms. He drew her closer as their lips met.

Yellow Bear's strange, Indian remedy had given him the full use of his right hand once again. Overwhelmed by gratitude, Chance turned to express his thanks.

"Thanks, Yellow . . ."

The sentence was never finished because the old warrior was nowhere to be found. While the two of them were lost in their joy and celebration, Yellow Bear had quietly slipped out the door unseen.

His work was done and he went on his way.

At that moment, Chance's understanding of the man began to grow. Chance had saved the Indian's life and in return, Yellow Bear healed his hand. According to the old warrior's abiding sense of honor, the debt was now paid. No further words between them were needed.

Puzzled by the Indian's sudden disappearance, her eyes wide as saucers, Amy looked around the room and then at Chance.

"Yellow Bear is very mysterious, isn't he?"

Chance nodded without comment.

It was then that her eyes spied something which hadn't been there before. "What is that?" she asked, pointing towards the door.

Right in front of the door, Yellow Bear had left a single eagle's feather.

Kneeling down next to the door, Chance pondered its meaning.

Yellow Bear had obviously left it there for a reason, perhaps as a signature or a symbol to mark his departure.

Since the Arapaho considered the eagle sacred, the one creature that flew the highest in God's sky, maybe the feather was left there to simply be a blessing on their home. Perhaps the feather was a sign that he would return to them someday.

It could be that the eagle's feather had a meaning known only to Yellow Bear. They had no idea. All that Chance knew for certain was that the Indian's friendship would be missed.

They wondered if they would ever see him again, but nothing was ever for certain in the West.

Chance stuck the feather in a small crack, just above the door frame, as a symbol of his anxiously awaited return.

Grabbing his hat and a box of shells, Chance paused at the door.

"I've got to go outside for a little while," he said. "If you need me, I'll be down at the old line shack."

Amy nodded, saying nothing, but taking note of the gun and extra shells.

As he saddled his horse, he noticed the day for the first time. It was the kind of day that makes a man glad to be alive.

The sun shone brightly, glowing like a giant ball of fire in the heavens. The sky was clear as the peal of a Sunday morning church bell and a man could see for a mile.

Chance had never seen a day so beautiful.

He knew his optimism might be caused by the regained use of his hand. Maybe it was the result of his reunion with Amy. Unable to pinpoint a single, specific reason, he simply rejoiced in the newfound sense of hope that this day offered.

Chance thought on all these things as he rode.

And then, almost as an afterthought, Chance realized how short-lived happiness might be, sometimes disappearing in a moment or a heartbeat. With a sudden burst of gunfire, Pete Ramsey could cause his entire world to come crashing down upon him. He had done it once before and he bitterly determined that it wouldn't happen again.

As long as Pete was free to roam the paths of this earth, unrestrained by shackles or the walls of a prison cell, their way of life would constantly be threatened. Chance's gun, and the ability to use it, was the only way he and Amy would ever know any lasting happiness.

Pete would come and Chance knew he must be ready.

He drew rein outside the weather-beaten, line shack and tethered his horse to a rail of the crumbling fence. The horse began to graze on the grass at his feet.

Realizing that he must be much faster when he faced Pete Ramsey, Chance placed some old whiskey bottles on the fence and began to practice. Minutes soon became hours as he worked on his draw. He was oblivious to the time, motivated and driven onward by a fierce desire to live.

The day had grown much hotter, as the merciless, noonday sun rained fire down upon him, leaving his throat as parched as a Texas dry spell. Chance went to the well and drew a cool bucket of water, drinking right from the bucket. As soon as he'd gotten his fill, he loaded his gun, ready for some more serious practice.

Chance stood in front of the broken-down, rail fence, hands at his side. Then he drew. This time, the gun sprang to his hand so quickly that it nearly startled him. Then he was firing, six shots taken and six broken bottles.

Ever since childhood, he had always been blessed with some natural skill with a six-gun. Skill and accuracy had never been a problem for him, but speed of hand had been. Now, thanks to many grueling hours of practice, his fast-draws were finally fast.

But still, Chance wasn't satisfied.

He placed some new bottles on the fence, which brought a smile to his face. Chance knew there would be no shortage of targets, because he'd guzzled plenty of whiskey.

Although Amy remained behind at the house, she slipped outside on the porch to see if she could hear the sounds of Chance practicing in the distance. After several minutes of concentration, she finally heard it.

The sound of gunfire was faint, almost undistinguishable to a person not expecting to hear anything.

As much as she hated to admit it, it brought a smile to her face. Chance's shooting was a welcomed sound, a hopeful one. It gave her husband a fighting chance to defend himself and face those evil men on their own terms.

The smile was certainly short-lived, her heart quaking in fear, wishing that Chance's practice wasn't necessary. And at the same time, she understood that his skill with a six-gun was essential to their survival.

No words had been spoken between them, because there had been nothing to say. Amy would have preferred that Chance stay clear of Pete Ramsey, but her desires did absolutely nothing to alter their situation.

It was only a matter of time until Pete would return to Boot Hill Valley with blood in his eyes, seeking to avenge his cousin's death. And when that time came, Amy knew her husband must fight or die.

Amy knew her man well.

Chance McBride was a man who fiercely honored the badge and strived to uphold the oath he took upon receiving it. He also believed strongly in all it represented.

Boot Hill Valley was his town and he believed its protection rested squarely on his shoulders. Pete Ramsey must be defeated and her husband would be the one who tried to stop him. A lesser man might have run, but Chance had never been numbered alongside the weak.

Amy even mulled over the idea of asking him to leave town, but she knew it would be futile to even speak of it. The man was stubborn, stubborn as the narrow-headed mule that once belonged to her father.

Courageous?

He was that also, never backing down from any challenge or obstacle. These were the qualities which made Chance what he was and she would have him to be no different. In fact, it had been these same characteristics which first endeared him to her those many years ago.

Yet she wondered what might happen to her if Chance failed. She shuddered at the idea of Pete, a man capable of the worst sort of evil imaginable, touching her. Even thinking about it made her skin crawl.

She quickly dismissed the thought, unwilling to tempt faint, refusing to even let the idea take root in her mind.

It was then she once again heard the faint sound of her husband practicing with his six-gun, a once-fearful sound which now gave her hope.

"Chance has to win," she muttered softly, while returning back into the house. "He has to."

Chapter Ten

Chance continued to practice with the well-worn revolver, the mountains resounding with the flurry of his gunfire.

Frogs were creaking in the lake nearby and crickets chirped their tunes in the grass nearby. These were common sounds around the lonely line shack, peaceful ones. But today, their usually-welcomed clamors would go unnoticed, victims of a six-gun's repeated voice.

After placing bottles on the fence, Chance reloaded once more. He returned to his place in front of the target, hands at his side. He closed his eyes and conjured up the image and memory of Pete Ramsey on the day of the attack, reaching for his gun. Upon seeing Pete reach for his gun in his mind, Chance grabbed iron and fired, shattering another bottle.

He reholstered the gun and repeated the sequence over and over again, until the gun was empty. This process continued for another hour.

Later, as he sat and rested next to the well, he heard the sound of a horse's hoof, kicking against a stone. Without thinking, almost instantaneously, the gun appeared in his fist.

"Chance," the voice rang out.

At the sound of Amy's voice, he holstered the gun.

"Chance, you've been up here for hours. I just came to see if you were all right."

Red-faced, Chance said, "I kind of lost track of time."

"It is getting kind of late in the day and we need some things from the store," Amy explained. "I didn't want to go by myself."

"Sorry about that." Chance walked over and embraced the woman, holding her tightly, yet softly, before leaning down to plant a kiss on her lips. "I'd be plumb tickled to death to be seen escorting the most handsome woman this side of the Mississippi."

Amy smiled and playfully swatted him away.

"Don't you even be thinking all your sweet talk is going to get you out of hot water with me, Chance McBride."

"I guess it was worth a try."

Chance knew it was time to step back into his rightful place, standing behind the sparkle of a pinned-on marshal's badge. Doc Arnold had waited long enough for his decision. But this time, the townspeople would be in for a surprise. No longer would they need to settle for half a peace officer. He was completely healed, sober, and his gun hand in its best shape ever.

"And I've got some business of my own, Amy, to take care of once we get to town."

Amy's eyes softened as she realized what was on his mind.

"Are you sure you're ready, Chance?"

Chance hand flashed for his gun, firing at one of the remaining bottles. The first slug split the bottle, sending its neck high into the air. Another shot shattered the neck, as his third slug broke one of the smaller pieces before it hit the ground.

Amy just smiled and anything else she might have been thinking went unsaid.

He quickly ejected the spent shells, reloaded, and mounted his horse.

"Let's go, Amy," he said, reining his horse around. "I'm ready as I ever will be, I guess."

* * *

A bone-weary cow horse ambled down the streets of Boot Hill Valley. Its gaunt and bony features cast a long shadow as it was coaxed along, nearly played-out from too many miles of travel in too short a time.

Yet the tired horse continued plodding on, mindful of the nearby livery stable, where a gentle rub-down and a bait of oats awaited him.

Its nostrils flared slightly and the horse's pace quickened, as it recognized the familiar scent of water coming from a nearby horse trough. But the rider pulled back hard against the reins, always an individual who wished to impose his will upon any mount and establish his own sense of dominance.

The horse was ridden by a lean-framed man, cowered slightly from many weeks in the saddle. His hat was pulled down low and its brim cast a shadow, which hid his face from the immediate view of all those around him.

As he rode down the street, the cowhand's eyes roamed from side to side, searching each doorway, window, and storefront, giving at least a fleeting, momentary attention on the purpose for which he'd been sent.

As he deliberately held back the reins of the thirsty horse, a mounted passerby gave the horse and rider a second glance, but continued on his way, figuring the scraggly pair of drifters merited no more of his interest.

Jason Ramsey breathed deeply, pleased that he hadn't been recognized.

It is much too early, he thought. *There will be time for McBride later, but first a drink. And then . . . a woman.*

He dismounted and tied his horse to the hitching post, next to the water trough.

The horse nickered softly and despite the nearby water, stretched out his neck and only scarcely missed taking a bite from the rider's shoulder.

As he climbed up the steps and stepped on the boardwalk, Jason heard the sound of piano music and pushed through the batwing doors.

One of the door's hinges creaked loudly, damaged nearly two years ago by a typical Saturday night brawl. The door's sudden squeak, generally ignored by the saloon's patrons, somehow drew one dance hall girl's attention. She gasped as she stared into the familiar eyes of Jason Ramsey and dropped a tray full of beer mugs.

"Jason," she exclaimed to no one in particular.

The saloon grew silent as a graveyard at midnight. Seemingly frozen in place, nobody moved or spoke, startled by the early, unexpected return of Jason Ramsey.

Nearly everyone in the saloon knew about the death of Ramsey's cousin and that Chance had been responsible for Padgitt's death. And if Jason was here now, it was certain Pete Ramsey wouldn't be too far behind.

Douglas Watkins, the undertaker, had been enjoying a peaceful drink at the saloon. But when Jason arrived, his thirst suddenly left him and he remembered that he didn't have enough coffins prepared. No doubt business would be picking up soon. Despite having taken only two sips of his beer, he set down his mug on the table and raced for the door.

Regaining her composure, the dance hall girl stooped down and began cleaning up the mess she made.

Jason delighted in seeing the sudden flurry of activity that his arrival caused. Proudly, he doubted that the arrival his older brothers, Pete or Duke, could have caused any more of a response.

He hitched up his gunbelt and swaggered over towards the bar. Slapping his hand down on the counter, he said, "Whiskey, barkeep."

Tossing that one down, he ordered the bartender to pour him another.

With the possible exception of a few assorted whispers and the hasty exit of several customers, the bar was still largely silent.

Jason turned around, elbows resting on the bar, and looked around the room. "This town isn't very lively anymore since I left," he bellowed. "Let's get the party started. There's no need to wait for Pete."

The piano player, still stricken with fear, did not move.

Jason stared hard in his direction and he could feel the man's eyes bearing down upon him.

"Are you going to play that contraption," he said, "or just going to keep roosting on the stool?"

Nervously, he began to play, hitting several wrong notes as he started.

* * *

After dropping off Amy at the dry goods store, Chance went to see Doc Arnold to inform him of his decision. The doctor was at his office.

"I've thought about what you said, Doc, and I'm here to take the job."

Arnold reached into the upper desk drawer and removed an envelope with Chance's name scrawled across the front, sliding it across the desk to him.

Opening the envelope, Chance saw that there was a badge inside, along with enough cash to pay his first month's salary.

"Pretty confident I'd take the job, weren't you?"

"Never had a doubt," he said with a smile. Then his eyes settled on the six-gun, resting on his hip. "Something's changed with you, hasn't it? I haven't seen you wear that gun in over three years."

After the doctor poured them two cups of coffee, Chance sat back in his chair and took his time sharing the story of Yellow Bear and the Indian's remedy.

Upon hearing Chance's incredible story, the doctor just shook his head.

"As much as we like to think we know it all, doctors simply don't have all the answers," Arnold said. "With every passing day, we are presented with changing ideas, new approaches, and innovative cures. A physician must be constantly learning, because medicine in always changing.

"A lot of my colleagues back East would simply call them savages. But for all their primitive ways, the Indians may still be more advanced than us in some fields of medicine. Their herbal remedies have been in use for hundreds of years," he continued. "And they actually work."

"Stories such as yours, Chance, always bring me to the same conclusion. As much as we like to brag about our skills and advancements, we just don't know it all."

Chance downed the last of his coffee and pinned the badge on his vest. "Well, Doc, I'd better start earning my pay. I'll talk to you later."

"By the way," Doc Arnold said, "that badge looks good back there."

"It feels good too."

The badge gleamed brightly in the evening sun as he left the doctor's office. He started towards the saloon, but a sudden thought came to his mind, something which caused Chance to pause in the middle of the street. He returned to his horse and removed the rifle from off his saddle.

The more Chance thought about it, he saw no reason for everybody in town to know about Yellow Bear and the information he just shared with the doctor. If it came down to a gunfight, it wouldn't hurt to have the element of surprise in his favor.

Most everybody in town knew about the ones he shot with a Winchester, back at the burial on Boot Hill. But absolutely nobody in town was expecting Chance to have any skill with a six-gun.

Chance was positive the doctor wouldn't tell anyone about their conversation and he decided it might be best to just leave it that way.

Now carrying his rifle, Chance once again started down the street. Passing in front of the store, he could see through the windows that Amy was still busy inside.

It seemed like the perfect time for him to start his rounds at the saloon.

As he walked towards the saloon, his spurs clanked loudly on the wooden floor boards. A dog came walking towards him and began to wag his tail as Chance approached. He stooped down to pet the animal and then continued on his way, glad to be back on the job.

Once outside the saloon doors, he paused, remembering the past three years and the shame that his behavior and this establishment brought upon him. The last time he was there, Chance made a fool of himself, begging the customers for drinks.

Hearing the music from inside immediately brought to his mind the desire for another drink. The sounds of piano music, the smell of cigarette smoking, and the noise from card games and loud conversations, all of it made him want another shot of liquor.

Chance licked his lips.

He now had a pocketful of money, more cash than he had ever known at one time the past three years. Unlike before, there would hardly be any limit to the whiskey he could buy for himself.

Just as Chance finally convinced himself that there could be no real harm in taking just one little drink, he thought of his wife, Amy.

Even with Yellow Bear's remedy for his hand, he knew there was no way a drunken marshal could protect his wife or possibly hope to stop Pete Ramsey and his brothers.

Chance stood outside the saloon doors, summoning up his courage and fighting back his gnawing, lustful urge for a bottle.

Inside, Jason Ramsey was leaning on the bar, tossing down whiskey and sizing up the dance hall girls, deciding which one he wanted to take upstairs later.

At nearly the same time, Chance gathered himself and was nearly ready to enter the saloon, a young, sandy-haired kid passed him by on the street.

"How are you doing, Marshal McBride?" he said, loudly.

At the sound of the name, Jason's head turned towards the door and he forgot about the whiskey and the women. Venom filled his soul. Jason could think of nothing other than his hatred for the marshal, the glory he'd earn for killing him, and of winning the praise of his older brothers when the deed was done.

At that precise moment, a newcomer to the town, wearing a bowler hat, chose to enter the saloon through its swinging doors, walking in directly behind Chance.

Jason Ramsey's eyes lit up as he saw the hated face of the marshal.

McBride will have no warning, he thought, *nothing to give him an edge. Besides, even with that rifle he's carrying, the fool doesn't even have a good gun hand.*

And with that one mistaken notion dominating his mind, combined with the effects of the liquor, Jason's hand reached for his gun.

Chapter Eleven

The newcomer's bad sense of timing could have placed him right square in the path of a bullet. But the fates chose to smile on the man, for it was his own clumsiness which would ultimately save his life.

Just as Chance started to shove his way through the batwing door, the doors swung right back and struck the newcomer in the shoulder. The force of the swinging doors knocked him off balance, carrying him free of the bullet's deadly, unyielding path.

Ramsey's first slug struck the left batwing door, showering them both with splinters and leaving a gaping hole through the wood. With scarcely a moment's thought, Chance's left hand grasped the startled patron's shirt front, and threw him to the safety of the wooden floorboards.

Once on the floor, the newcomer in the bowler hat covered his head with one arm and tried to keep out of the line of fire.

In the meantime, Jason's gun flamed again and a slug barely creased Chance's left side.

By this time, Chance threw the rifle to his shoulder and was levering a pair of shots at the outlaw.

His first shot struck Jason just a couple of inches above his belt, turning his shirt a growing shade of crimson. But it failed to stop the young outlaw, who dug in his heels and continued firing.

Chance's second slug caromed upward off Jason's belt buckle, leaving a bloody furrow across his lips. The lips, curled in rage, were now marred by a bullet. Between curses, he spat away blood.

The force of the rifle slug hitting him caused Jason's next slug to go off target, striking the newcomer's hat, leaving a large, dark hole in the crown of the man's bowler. The customer crouched lower on the floor, covering his head with both arms.

Once more, desperate to kill the marshal, Jason triggered another shot.

At the report of the gun, something tore through the fabric on the marshal's shirt sleeve, but Chance levered the rifle again, his last shot striking its mark . . .

In his final desperate moments, Jason realized the fatal mistake he made. He expected McBride to be unarmed or unable to fire, an easy target for a cold-blooded murder. But most foolish of all, Jason figured his sudden ambush would kill the marshal long before McBride ever realized he was under attack.

There at the end, Jason could see everything so clearly, as if reality was slowed far beneath its usual speed. He saw the marshal's lean frame in a fighting posture, his tin star sparkling brightly in the saloon's lights.

Jason's lips uttered another oath, as the marshal squeezed the trigger once more. The Winchester sprouted flame as the powerful slug found its target.

Something struck Jason wickedly and he clutched at the dreadful, searing pain in his chest. It was then he saw the smoke from the rifle and finally heard the gun's report. While still trying to speak, he slumped over on the floor, face down.

Chance rushed over to his attacker and knelt down beside him.

"Someone get Doc Arnold," he said. "Hurry."

One of the saloon's customers nodded and sprinted out the door.

As Chance rolled Jason over on his back, he immediately knew that the doctor, if he arrived on time, would be able to do nothing for him. Ramsey struggled to speak, sensing that his time on this earth would be short.

Someone handed the marshal a canteen and he gently placed it to Ramsey's trembling lips, doing whatever he could to bring some sense of relief to his final moments.

After a couple of brief swallows, Jason hoarsely said, "Thanks for the drink. I almost had you, McBride."

The marshal nodded. "You came mighty close."

He smiled at the statement. After a moment's pause and a grimace from the pain, he added, "Pete told me to wait, but I wanted to make him proud."

"I'm sure he would have been."

At Chance's remark, Jason managed another smile, but then his eyes closed in death, beckoned by the ancients.

"So long, boy," McBride said softly.

Chance rose and walked away from Jason's fallen body, not speaking, but thumbing shells into his rifle as he moved.

Chance paused just inside the saloon doors. Standing there, brushing off the dirt from himself was the newcomer who Chance shoved to the floor.

Extending his hand, the newcomer said, "Thank you, marshal. It would appear that you saved my life."

Chance shook his hand. "Glad I could help."

"Is it all over, marshal?"

"Yes, I think so," Chance said. "For now."

"For now? That sounds kind of ominous, marshal. Whatever do you mean?"

"The trouble's over for now," McBride said, pointing towards Jason's body, "but that kid over there has a couple of brothers. They won't take it well."

"Ahh, I see."

The man spoke with a distinctive British accent and it was obvious that he had only been in this country for a short time. He reached down to pick up his hat and stuck a finger through the bullet hole in his derby hat.

"This used to be a good hat," he said.

"You're lucky, friend. That hole could have been through your head."

"You're so right, my good man. You're so right."

Chance pushed back the hat and scratched his head. "If you don't mind me asking, you don't sound like you're from around here, stranger."

"Yes, that's true, marshal. I am from London. My name is Quentin Rigby Hawkins."

"Pleased to meet you," Chance said. "That's a mighty big handle for a man to tote around."

He smiled.

"I first came to this country nearly a year ago," Hawkins said. "I had heard so many stories of the American West, I just had to see it for myself." He replaced the damaged brown bowler on the top of his head. "Thus far, it has lived up to all my expectations."

"And it almost got you killed."

"It shall leave me with an outstanding story to tell, should I ever choose to return to London. And for that I owe you my life. Until such a time as I can return the favor, I am at your service, marshal.

"It's not that I'm not grateful for your offer, Mr. Hawkins, but you'll be doing me a bigger favor if you just keep your head down,"

The Englishman nodded. "As you wish, marshal. Thank you again."

Trouble and death are never without spectators, for a man is often morbidly attracted to witness the tragedy of others. Boot Hill Valley was no exception.

The gunfight created quite a commotion in this once-peaceful town. As Chance pushed through the batwing doors and walked out of the saloon, a crowd of people came running up the street, curious about this latest round of gunplay.

Amy was among them.

Unlike the others in the street, hers was not a desire to feast on another's misfortune. Amy was driven by fear. She merely wished to learn if misfortune had already befallen her, by taking the life of her precious husband.

Amy rushed towards the saloon, one hand holding up her skirt as she ran, fearful of what her eyes might see when she arrived. But even then, her heart could not bear to receive the grim news from even a well-meaning friend. If something happened to Chance, Amy knew she must see and learn of it for herself.

Her reddened, tear-stained eyes filled with love and relief when they met his. Amy's heart leaped within her.

"Oh, Chance," she exclaimed, sobbing. "I'm so glad you're not hurt."

Her arms reached out to him.

"Yep, I'm fine," he said, trying to calm her fears. "It was Jason Ramsey. He tried to ambush me when I walked into the saloon. I guess he wasn't good enough."

As Amy embraced him, Chance was suddenly gripped by the cold realization that, from this moment on, there could be no turning back. The die had been cast. Two of Pete's kin had died by his hand.

There would be no forgiveness for his actions, no willingness to look the other way, nor would there be any desire to set them aside to

105

the past. Fate had chosen to place this dreadful chain of events into motion. And nothing would alter its course . . .

Nothing but the death of Pete Ramsey.

Or Chance McBride.

After spending several minutes reassuring Amy of his immediate safety, she finally consented to return to her shopping. And it was then that Chance made his way to the hardware store.

Walking down the street, Chance was greeted with an equal smattering of smiles and harsh stares, some of the townsfolk happy with his return and others doubting the ability of a drunken and crippled marshal to adequately defend their town.

Obviously, the word had already gotten around Boot Hill Valley that they now had a new marshal.

Or an old marshal anew.

No doubt some of them couldn't wait for the next town meeting, which would give them a chance to vocally register their displeasure with the latest hiring choices of the town fathers.

Mr. Howard, the store's owner, was just outside the shop, placing some lady's order into a buckboard. He smiled as Chance drew closer, making note of the marshal's rifle and also the fact, he now had a six-gun strapped to his hip.

"Howdy, marshal. I heard you had some trouble at the Angel's Roost," he said, hoping for some first-hand details of the gun fight.

Chance removed his hat, wiping the sweat from the headband before returning it to his head. "It sure is a hot one," he muttered, largely ignoring the storekeeper's question.

Howard finished loading the supplies and Chance offered to help, shouldering a bag of flour. The storekeeper waved to the lady as she drove away.

"Is it true, marshal? Did you really kill Jason Ramsey?"

"It's true."

"Good."

"It won't make Pete happy."

"And I won't ever be happy," Howard said, "until every single one of those Ramsey brothers are planted out in Boot Hill."

Howard walked back into the store with Chance following him.

"Doc Arnold said you'd never use a six-gun again," Howard said, fishing for an explanation. "You use that rifle?"

"Yes, Mr. Howard. I used the rifle."

"You're getting pretty good with that thing, aren't you?"

"Better than you know."

Sam Howard didn't mean anything by his questions, so Chance wasn't particularly bothered by them. In fact, he was rather amused by the interest.

Howard was just an old man, with old ways, needing something to be the first to talk about with all his friends.

Boot Hill Valley was a small town, so a gunfight was obviously a noteworthy event, a serious matter to be discussed and gossiped about.

Sam just didn't want to be the last one to get all the facts. Being nosy was part of Sam's nature and few things happened in town that escaped his attention.

Already wise to Howard's manner, Chance decided to toy with him a little, by saying nothing more about the shooting. In doing so, he deliberately infuriated the shopkeeper, further serving to pique his innate sense of curiosity.

"What can I get for you today," he grumbled, "since you aren't in a mood for friendly conversation?"

Chance smiled innocently. "I could use about a thousand rounds of ammunition."

"That's a lot of bullets, marshal. You planning to start a war?" Howard asked, as he started to grab them from the shelf.

"No, I'm just looking to survive a war if one gets started."

Howard quoted the price for the merchandise and Chance fished into his pocket for the money he owed him.

While carrying the additional rounds of ammunition, Chance walked outside the hardware store and was startled when he looked up to check the sky.

Off in the distance, high above the mountain tops, he saw a dazzling flash of lightning streak across the sky. The lightning was soon followed by a booming blast of thunder, which caused a couple of the horses, tied to the hitching rail out front, to rear into the air and jerk upon their reins.

He spoke softly to the horses, which seemed to calm their fears.

As Chance started back down the street to locate his wife, he felt the first sprinkles begin to fall upon his shoulders.

Then the rain began to fall.

A fierce and chilly wind gusted down the street. Chance paused long enough to pull his hat down tighter over his head.

The storm started out as little more than a drizzle, quickly becoming stronger and more forceful, until the rains eventually became a torrential downpour.

It was then the skies completely let loose.

Chapter Twelve

Morning found Chance working at the marshal's office, doing some minor repairs to the office, sweeping up, and checking out the wanted posters.

He was truly glad to be back on the job.

The rain, which was now pouring down from the clouds in bucketfuls, continued falling throughout the night and still hadn't stopped.

Chance's wet coat and hat hung from a peg on the wall, over in the corner, water still dripping from the garments, darkening the wooden floorboards beneath them and finding its way down through the cracks.

A bucket sat off to one side of the room, catching the dripping water from a leak in the roof. Chance had already dumped the bucket twice since his arrival.

The marshal took another drink of his coffee and grumbled at his inability to make a decent pot.

Amy was still sleeping, so he hadn't bothered to wake her before he left the house that morning. Now, he was trying to get by on what he could brew and he was having a mighty rough time of it. His coffee was strong enough to dissolve iron and black as old Satan himself.

He walked over to the window, took a look outside, and saw that the rain didn't in any way appear to be slackening. As much as they needed the rain, he prayed the worst of it would let up soon.

Increasingly, Yellow Bear was at the center of his thoughts and Chance wondered what became of the Indian. Their time together had been much too short.

Chance yearned to see him again, to talk to him, to learn more about the old Arapaho warrior.

Yellow Bear was out there somewhere, searching for a world in which he would have the freedom to live as he saw fit, a world every free man seeks.

That was the reason why he fled the reservation.

Living as he saw fit, it was also a pursuit that Chance knew all too well. But he also learned a man will never find any freedom in a bottle.

In a relatively short time, he and Yellow Bear had become trusted friends. Thrown together in circumstances that allowed them to help each other, their lives had obviously been intertwined by some strange twist of fate.

True friendships can never be severed by the miles. And although he didn't know why, Chance was certain their paths would cross again.

As he stared off into the storm outside the window, another thought was preying on his mind.

Pete would be here soon.

Chance knew it would be impossible to avoid a violent confrontation between them. Pete hated him and wanted revenge. Chance wanted to protect Amy and the town.

Strong and bitter feelings such as those the two men held for each other can only lead to trouble and bloodshed. And when they met again, it was inevitable that one or both of them must die at the other's hand.

A clap of thunder jolted Chance from his thoughts. He walked over to the bucket which was catching water from the leaky roof. It was nearly full.

He grabbed the bucket, opened the door, and tossed the contents outside. Fighting the strength of the wind, he tugged the door shut, and returned the bucket to its place.

Drip, drip, drip, the water began making a small metallic clank as it once again began to fill from the storm.

Pete was surely on his way back to Boot Hill Valley by now. Chance was sure of it, for every nerve in his body was warning him of danger. Hell was coming. And it would be here soon.

As he listened to the water drip into the metal bucket, Chance realized that he was growing tired of the waiting and wondering.

Let him come, Chance thought.

Then he remembered the line shack. He decided if the rain would ever let up, he needed to do some more gun practice for the eventual fight that was surely coming to Boot Hill Valley.

But for now, there was something he must do first. Chance's stomach was grumbling, reminding him that it was time for some breakfast. Grabbing his still-damp coat and hat, he decided that he would brave the weather for some breakfast.

Going outside with rifle in hand, Chance lowered his head against the harsh wind and the bitter onslaught of rain. Leaving the comfort of the boardwalks, he started down the steps toward the street.

As he started to cross over to the diner, Chance carefully slogged through the muddy pit, as small but ever-growing streams of water began flowing down what used to be a city street.

For just a moment, Chance wondered if the muddy ordeal of chasing after breakfast would be worth all his effort. Another chilly gust of wind almost swept the hat from his head and he remembered the one thing which might make it all worthwhile.

The diner always served a hot and decent cup of coffee.

* * *

Startled from her sleep by the fury of the rain upon the steel roof and a frightening burst of thunder, Amy reached over to the nearby pillow and saw that her husband was already gone into town and performing his duties as marshal.

Amy rose from her bed, lit the coal oil lamp, and began dressing to face the day. Checking her reflection in the mirror, while combing last night's sleep from her hair, she was finally pleased with the result.

She threw a couple more logs in the stove and began preparing a fresh pot of coffee, something Chance was certain to want when he returned to the house out of this downpour.

The scent of fresh coffee and breakfast cooking in the skillet filled the room as a gentle knock sounded on the door. The knock startled Amy and she rushed to grab the rifle and levered a shell up into the chamber.

"Who is it?" she shouted.

Unsure if there was truly no answer to her question, or perhaps the sound of the response was covered over by the raging storm, Amy called out again.

Still no answer.

Amy walked to the door, unlocked it, and leveled her gun on the doorway. Her every nerve was on edge and a tense finger rested on her trigger.

"Come on in," she shouted. "And come in slowly."

The door opened slowly and in the darkness she saw Yellow Bear standing outside in the rain, but he appeared to have no horse with him.

"Yellow Bear," she said, earing back the hammer and lowering her rifle. "Please, sir, come in."

The warrior walked inside the house, with only the slightest bit of water dripping from his clothes and long gray hair. Looking at the man, Amy was bewildered that the Indian wasn't absolutely soaking wet after being outside for only the briefest time in the brutal storm.

Amy had no explanation for his state, yet she feared to ask the old Indian about it.

Yellow Bear simply looked at her and said, "Doesn't McBride's Woman know the eagle flies above the rain?"

Amy didn't reply to his question. She barely knew what to say, since the old Arapaho had seemingly read her mind once again. She wondered where he'd been since the last time they saw hm.

"Like the wind, I come, I go."

Unsure of what else to say and fearful of thinking about anything else he might perceive, she finally said, "Please sit down here at the table. Would you care for some coffee?"

"Yellow Bear would like that?" he said, taking a seat.

While pouring another cup of coffee, Amy decided that she would just go ahead and speak to the Indian freely about whatever came to mind. Why shouldn't she? Thus far, she sure hadn't succeeded in hiding anything from him.

She handed him the steaming cup of liquid and he proceeded to drink down half of it, like the coffee wasn't even warm.

"Good coffee, McBride's Woman."

"Thank you, Yellow Bear," she said, bringing the coffee pot over to the table and taking a place at the table beside him. "How is it that an Indian comes to like coffee?"

"The White missionaries shared it with me when I was a young one, learning to read their Holy Book." He drank down the rest of his hot coffee as if drinking water from a running stream. "How is McBride?"

"His hand is fine," Amy replied, refilling his cup.

"I didn't ask about his hand. How is McBride?"

"But, Yellow Bear, you healed his hand," she said, taking a sip of her own coffee. "We owe you everything for that."

"I do nothing for McBride's hand. He suffered only from a broken spirit."

"What do you mean?" Amy said. "I saw you cut my husband's hand with your knife and the next day the incision was gone. Are you really trying to tell me that your magic had nothing to do with that?"

Yellow Bear smiled. "I thought you Whites had no belief in magic."

"Well, I don't," Amy said. "But I saw you do your magic . . . or healing—or whatever you did to my husband. All I know is that he is better now."

"I knew it would be so. I saw he killed the young one named Ramsey."

"You saw that?"

"McBride's Woman, the eagle sees everything."

"Well, thank you for healing him."

"I did not heal him. McBride healed himself."

Amy was beside herself, trying to fully understand the conversation.

"Your White doctors cannot heal a broken or wounded spirit. That is what I did for McBride." He quickly tossed down the second cup of hot coffee. "McBride's spirit was damaged, but no longer. He now has the spirit of the eagle. That is all McBride or any man needs to live."

Amy leaped from her chair and embraced the old warrior. "I'm not fully sure I understand all of this, Yellow Bear, but I will never forget what you did for us. And I will always be in your debt."

"You are a strong woman. McBride chose well."

"Thank you."

"I must go now,' Yellow Bear said.

"Before you go, I must ask you a question."

"And what is your question, McBride's Woman?"

"You left behind a feather the last time you were here, the one sticking above the door. What does it mean?"

"What makes you think the feather means anything? Sometimes an eagle just loses a feather, like you lose a hair."

"So, you're saying the feather meant nothing?"

"I did not say that."

Amy was growing frustrated by their conversation. "Then what are you saying?"

"Eagles have great power. Their feathers are what allow them to soar above the earth and touch the Great Spirits. They cannot fly without them. So, if an eagle has left one at your door, great honor and power have been bestowed upon you.

"It could be that the feather was left here to be seen by the Wolf and the Raven, so they could know this place was protected by the eagle. McBride's Woman must know the feather can be many things."

"If the eagle really knows all things, then you had to know that my husband wasn't home now. So, why did you come here, Yellow Bear?"

"I could not go into town, but I wished to warn McBride that the one named Ramsey is now coming for him," Yellow Bear said. "I have seen them riding this way. Brother Wolf has seen them too. I knew McBride's Woman would wish to tell him."

Yellow Bear said nothing more, opening the door and going out into the rain.

Amy stood in the doorway and watched him go, but once again, the old warrior seemed to suddenly disappear from her sight.

As she closed and locked the door behind him, her first instinct was to blame this disappearance on her inability to see through the driving rain. But only for an instant did she even entertain the notion that Yellow Bear was telling the truth and that the Indian somehow returned to his form as an eagle.

Quickly dismissing the whole idea from her mind, she looked down upon the floor and gasped at what she saw.

On the floor, just next to her feet was another eagle's feather, which she also stooped down to pick up and place next to the other one, above the door.

And not too far down the road from McBride's house, the flood waters were bursting out of the mountains, torrents of water pouring through Boot Hill, as they had been for the past twelve hours.

As this growing river of water and mud plowed through the cemetery, it disturbed a recently-buried soul from savoring his eternal rest. His firmly-constructed pine casket began to float upon the flood waters, pried up from its former place underneath the sod.

Now fully carried along by the raging force of the waters, this one wooden casket was soon joined by another and another, a growing river of the dead, headed on their way towards Boot Hill Valley.

Chapter Thirteen

A vast cloud of dust was formed, stirred up by the hoof falls of a half dozen, determined riders. These were hard-bitten men, tough, dangerous, and well-suited for violence.

Their horses were not being pushed beyond their limits of endurance, for there was no real need for urgency. A man's life can always be taken at one's leisure.

But taking a man's life was precisely what they had in mind.

Not wanting to be trampled by their hoofs, a lazy cottontail scrambled to get out of the way of the approaching horses. The clamor of their approach also sent any number of frightened birds and squirrels fleeing from them.

Pete Ramsey and his brother, Duke, had gotten their beeves to the railhead without incident. And now they were on their way back to Boot Hill Valley to rejoin their brother, Jason. Four other riders accompanied them on their return for home.

Pete's clothes were stained with hundreds of miles of sweat and trail dust, his boots filthy from cow manure and horse droppings. His hollow, unshaven jaws hadn't recently been introduced to the use of a straight razor.

In short, Pete's manner of appearance was, for the most part, about the same as usual.

Duke, on the other hand, took on more of the looks of an Eastern gentleman. Despite his time on the trail, his boots shined brightly and his clothes were fresh and clean. His face was clean-shaven, and if he removed his hat, a person would scarcely notice even one hair out of place.

Duke's cleanliness had become sort of a joke among the other drovers, a routine matter for laughter and discussion. Some of them even called him a dandy.

One of the other drovers recently suggested that trail dust steered a wide path around Duke, even when he was riding drag. Duke even laughed at that one himself.

But in spite of the humor at Duke's expense, there was also a caution and reserve to the drovers' wisecracks. They all knew of the man's dangerous nature and had a healthy respect for it, so the jokes and prodding never got too far out of hand.

"If this good weather holds up, we ought to reach town by nightfall," Duke said.

"There ain't no hurry, Duke," Pete explained, his tobacco-stained teeth bared in a vicious grin. "McBride will die just as easy tomorrow as he would today. And besides, I don't want to rush the job," he added. "I want him to die slow and painful."

As they approached a small stream, Pete motioned at the others to stop and water their horses. A couple of the men stooped down and began to fill their canteens. Some drank directly from the stream. Others just splashed the cool water on their necks and faces, hoping to remove the dust which accumulated as they rode.

Pete dismounted and sat down on a rock, leisurely beginning to roll a smoke. When finished, he took a deep, long puff before hollering for the others to join him.

The other riders quickly began to filter away from the stream, soon forming a small circle around him. While they waited, a couple of them smoked. Another pair filled their jaws with tobacco.

"I'm glad you boys decided to come along," Pete said, nodding over at his brother. "Me and Duke can handle McBride all by ownselves, but we might need a little help drinking the town's whiskey and dancing with their ladies." He flicked the cigarette butt into the stream. "I trust you boys are up to the job."

Pete's remark was greeted with cheers and howls of laughter.

"But one more thing," Pete added. "Don't anyone touch McBride's woman." A cunning gleam could be seen in his eyes. "I'm planning to slap my own brand on that one myself."

"And I'm gonna put a bullet right between the eyes of old Doc Arnold," Duke said. "I never did like him. But I won't kill him until I make that sanctimonious old codger beg for his life."

Isaac Cox was a huge man, with a massive chest and shoulders. Cruelty was a trait that he lived for, constantly bullying others throughout his life. "I don't care what you boys do," he said. "All I want is the whiskey."

Duke removed a watch from his pocket and opened it up to check the time. "It's getting late, Pete. And besides, that sky out of ahead of us is looking pretty dark. We might be riding into a bad storm."

Pete sauntered over to his horse and slung himself into the saddle. The other ones in the party also started to climb atop their horses.

"Duke is right. We better be going," Pete said. "I'd like to get to the ranch before the sun goes down."

Duke mounted up and slapped the spurs to his horse. "Yes, let's ride."

Five hours later, six wet and miserable riders road up to the Ramseys' ranch house.

The bunch of them had just ridden through one of the worst storms they'd ever seen in Boot Hill Valley.

But despite the brutal rain, Pete thought it was strange that Jason hadn't come out of the house to greet them. Maybe the boy was still in town, he thought to himself. That must be it. The boy always did have a weakness for the ladies.

Pete and Duke dismounted outside of the ranch house. And instead of taking the time to stretch their weary bones, they quickly climbed the steps to get underneath the porch, somewhere warm and dry from the driving rain.

"Isaac," Duke shouted, "make sure our horses get put away."

Although he worked for the brothers, Cox grew rankled at the remark. Isaac also never grew accustomed to the idea of following orders. Under normal circumstances, he might have pushed the issue, but he knew he was no match for a gun battle with either of the two older brothers.

"Right away, boss," Cox said, the words almost catching in his throat.

After the Ramsey brothers were safely in the house and out of earshot, he added, "One of these days, you boys are going to get what you have coming."

Pete walked into the house, removed his hat, and hung it on a peg next to the door. Following his brother through the door, Duke did likewise. From there, Pete moved to the liquor cabinet and poured himself a glass of brandy.

"You care for some?" he said to his brother.

"Not right now, Pete. Thanks anyway. All I want to do is get into some dry clothes."

Duke carefully studied the room, his eyes darting from side to side. "There's something not right here," he mumbled to no one in particular.

"What did you say?" Pete asked, as he sat down.

"There's something wrong here. I don't know what it is, but I can sense it more than explain it to you."

Duke quickly sprinted up the stairs, skipping every other step. Once upstairs, he moved down the hallway, jerking open the doors and checking every single room. Jason was nowhere to be found. He cursed loudly, a profane string of oaths which were heard all the way downstairs.

When he returned to the staircase, Pete was waiting at the base of it. "What's eating you, boy," he asked.

"Jason's not here," Duke blurted out.

"I wouldn't worry about it."

"Well, you should," Duke said, bounding down the staircase.

"He's probably still in town right now," Pete muttered, "sitting at a table, with a cold brew in front of him and a warm woman beside of him."

Pete grinned at his remark, but Duke saw no humor in it.

"He's probably still in town, checking out the whores. He'll be back soon, Duke.

"No, he won't," Duke said, refusing to let the matter drop.

The urgency in his brother's tone was finally starting to capture Pete's attention. Duke was always the level-headed one. And if something had him this upset, Pete knew it was something worth hearing out.

"What are you talking about, Duke?" Pete said.

"Damn it, Pete. Something's not right here. None of Jason's things are laying around. His bed's not been slept in. There's not one thing here that would indicate that he's ever been back, not since we started pushing those beeves northward."

Pete stood there silently, the gravity of the situation finally beginning to dawn upon him. Worry lines began to grow on his forehead.

"Don't you remember? You sent him to check on McBride," Duke explained. "But even doing that, he should have made it back here by now.

"Pete, what if Jason ran into some trouble in town or on the way back here? Maybe he never even made it back." Duke said. "He might be hurt out there somewhere." Maybe worse." Duke paused suddenly, as he saw his words having their desired effect. "But what if he didn't listen to you, Pete? What if he just decided to tackle McBride all by himself?

The younger of the two brothers needed to say nothing more, for his statements sent Pete racing out the door and heading for the bunkhouse.

All of the Ramseys' employees had their accommodations in the main bunkhouse, including their Chinese cook, a short man named Lau Lee.

Initially upon Lau Lee's arrival, a number of the men objected to sharing their quarters with what they called a Chinaman. But most of the complaints fell silent or were quickly forgotten when Pete began to finger the butt of his Colt, while staring at them coldly.

As the door of their bunkhouse was brutally thrown open and nearly loosed from its hinges, Pete found himself staring into the barrels of several quickly-drawn revolvers.

But when the hands, a number of them wearing no more than long johns, saw who was at the door, they all holstered their guns. A couple of them looked embarrassed and fearful after almost putting a slug through Pete Ramsey, a man who was fast with a six-gun but had no sense of humor.

Pete stomped through the door, until he faced a couple of the men who stayed behind to care for the ranch.

"Have you boys seen Jason in the last couple of days?" Pete said.

"No, we surely ain't," Willie Picket said. "We figured he was still with you, off somewhere on the trail."

"No, I sent him back this way a few days ago, to take care of a little business for me. He should have made it back here to the ranch by now."

"There's been nobody in town for several days," Bill offered. "Nobody had any real reason to go."

Lau Lee interrupted them, his broken English sometimes difficult to understand, "I not cook for young Jason since you left. Maybe he not get back from Boot Hill Valley."

That was an ever-growing idea that Pete preferred not to consider. But it was also beginning to appear much more obvious to him and Duke that the Chinaman might be exactly right.

"Cox," Pete said, "I want you ready to ride in ten minutes. We're going to town."

After just getting back from his time on the trail, Isaac Cox had been busy peeling off his wet clothes, looking to put on something dry. Now, he bitterly realized that he would have to go back out in the pelting rain, just to find Pete's stupid, little brother.

Although Cox didn't have much use for Duke, he absolutely despised Jason, a man who routinely treated most of the hired hands like slaves, or something a man would scrape off the sole of his boots.

Pete charged back out of the bunkhouse, not even bothering to close the door behind him. Duke matched him, step-for-step. "What have you got in mind, Pete?"

"We're going to quietly slip into town and find out what happened to Jason," Pete said, going up the steps into the house.

"What if McBride killed him?" Duke said.

Pete went over and removed a rifle from the rack, a glint of satisfaction showing in his eyes. "Same as we already agreed. I'll shoot him full of holes. But if Jason's dead, we'll make sure the whole town pays for it, every single one of them."

When the two brothers came back outside, Isaac Cox was waiting just inside the warm, dry barn, standing alongside three saddled horses. He was leaning against one of the stalls, calmly smoking a cigarette.

Duke just stared at him. "What are you doing, Cox? Smoking in a barn, could it be that you just don't think or are you simply stupid?"

For a second, Cox just glared at him, saying nothing. "What do you mean, Duke? You ever try to light one in this kind of driving rain."

Perhaps because of his size or maybe the fact he was far and away their best ranch hand, Isaac Cox was still the only employee who ever dared to challenge an order from the Ramsey brothers.

"I don't care. It's still a good way to burn the entire place down. I'm telling you to get rid of that thing. Now."

Isaac simply scowled at him, carelessly flicking the butt outside into the rain.

"You happy now, Duke?"

"I'm telling you, Cox. Just don't start on me today."

Although he initially laughed it off, Pete had eventually come around to Duke's line of thinking. He found himself growing increasingly worried about what might have happened to Jason. And at that very moment, a petty dispute between a couple of people took a distant second place to his thoughts of fear and worry.

"Will you two shut up?" Pete said. "I've heard just about enough of you. Now get on your horses and let's ride."

Chapter Fourteen

Chance whistled a tune while he made his evening rounds, doing his best to stay out of the rain.

The Henry rifle that he carried was cocked and ready for whatever evil might befall him. And although things seemed mighty peaceful around town, Chance knew it wasn't going to last long.

There was a pot full of trouble simmering, quickly building its way to a full boil. Chance could feel it.

Turning into the Angel's Roost, he once again saw Quentin Rigby Hawkins, lingering at the bar.

Chance thought the man looked dashing in all his best, imported finery, but the marshal couldn't seem to hold back a chuckle upon seeing a bullet hole in Hawkins' expensive hat.

"Good evening to you, marshal."

Chance nodded. "Howdy, Mr. Hawkins. I could have sworn that I encouraged you to leave town. Why are you still here?"

Although he would have never admitted it to anybody, there was just something about this man that Chance liked. It was for that reason, the marshal had no desire for him to hang around and possibly catch a stray bullet.

McBride could also see no reason for a rather odd, but good man, to die, just because of some false sense of obligation to him.

Hawkins tossed down his drink. "The whiskey here is quite good," he said, looking for a moment at the ceiling. "As to my reason for not leaving Boot Hill Valley, I rather like it here. I suppose that is why, marshal."

Chance did his best to appear angry with the Englishman. "How would you like to end up on the losing end of another revolution?"

"Your people may have defeated my country in your Revolution," Hawkins said, "but that does not indicate that you have the personal wherewithal to eject me from your fair city."

The man from England had a little fire to him. A man ought to always hold a little pride in himself. Chance liked that.

"Now, don't you just bet on it," Chance said. "I always rise to a good challenge."

Hawkins smiled, greatly enjoying the back and forth with this American.

"I have done a great deal of sparring before I came to this country. And if I must say so myself, I believe I am quite good."

Chance laughed. "Unfortunately, the men who threaten this town are not gentlemen, men who fight fairly under a clearly-defined set of rules. These are hard and evil men, killers, ones who seldom fight with their fists. Most of their disputes are settled with a gun."

Hawkins merely smiled. "I am prepared for that as well."

It was then that Chance finally saw the man through new eyes.

At first appearance, Hawkins gave the impression of a well-bred, English gentleman, a person of great culture and refinement. And although it was indeed likely that he was all of these things, there was clearly another side to the man. There was a depth to him as well.

Hawkins was a proud man, tough, willing to face life on its own terms. A rugged country needed men such as him, ones who could adapt and grow with the land. In fact, Chance thought it likely that the colonists who took on the British were no doubt made up of men such as him.

"Quentin Rigby Hawkins," Chance said. "I'd be proud to buy you a drink."

"Why, thank you, marshal. I'd be honored to accept."

Chance called out to the bartender, who brought Hawkins another whiskey and the marshal only a beer.

"Marshal, you asked me why I hadn't left town and I believe I owe you a clear and civil response."

Chance sat down and sipped from his beer. "Go ahead, Mr. Hawkins."

"Liberty," he said.

Chance looked puzzled.

"When your thirteen colonies rebelled against the king, they claimed it was because of tyranny. Apparently, the colonials wanted to have freedom to live according to the dictates of their own hearts.

"You see, marshal, that is why I came to this country," Hawkins continued. "It was for freedom. That is also the reason I remained in town, even against your wishes."

Try as hard as he might, Chance could come up with no good reason to refute the gentleman. He made a powerful argument.

"Hawkins," Chance said, "if everyone from your country was hardheaded as you are, England might have won that war. And we'd probably be sitting down to tea right now."

Chance lifted his beer in a salute. "To freedom," he said.

Hawkins did the same. "To America."

* * *

Exhausted after a long day of work, Doctor Joseph Arnold thought he deserved a trip to the saloon for a quiet drink. It took some difficulty getting to the saloon, requiring him to cross over on horseback, because of nearly four inches of water that was running down the street.

As he tied his horse in the driest alley available, a brawny arm locked around his throat, cutting off any chance to cry for help.

The aged doctor kicked and struggled, but he was clearly no match for the steely arm of Isaac Cox, who dragged him through the water over to his office. Pete and Duke waited for them there.

Once they were all safely inside the doctor's office, Cox released his grip on Arnold's neck. He rubbed his throat and replied, "Welcome back, Pete. You too, Duke. And how was your trip?"

Pete got up from the doctor's own chair, walked across the room, and slapped the doctor across the mouth, splitting the doc's lower lip.

"That's just about enough smart mouth out of you, doc. I want to know what happened to my brother."

"He's dead, Pete. The marshal killed him last night."

"How did it happen?"

The doctor sad nothing as he rubbed his bloody lip and now-swollen jaw. Duke rushed over and struck him again.

"You heard my brother," Duke said, holding his cocked six-gun underneath the doctor's nose. "You answer him now."

"Jason was over drinking at the saloon," Arnold said, wiping the blood from his lip with the sleeve of his coat. "Could I have a drink?"

Pete looked disgusted, while still trying to digest the news about another member of his family dead. "Get the old man a drink."

Isaac found a bottle of whiskey on the counter, something that Arnold mostly used for cleaning wounds. He located a glass, blew out any dust, and poured it half full. Then he handed it to the doctor.

"Thanks, Isaac," he replied. After a quick swallow, the doctor continued, "When McBride walked into the saloon, Jason just started firing. Chance threw up his rifle and killed him."

"Are you saying that Jason fired first?" Pete said.

"That's exactly what I'm saying."

Duke flew into a rage. "You're a liar, old man!"

"No, Duke. I'm not lying. And please tell me what reason I'd have for doing so."

"Why didn't you do anything to save him?" Pete asked.

"Your brother was already dead when I got to the Angel's Roost. There was just nothing I could do."

"So, doc, you didn't actually see the fight. What makes you so sure that our brother drew first?"

"There were at least four or five witnesses to the shooting," Doc said. "It happened just the way I told you."

Isaac continued to stand next to the door, listening for movement outside the door, and making sure they had no unexpected guests.

"I swear I'll kill McBride," Pete said. "I'll kill him."

"No, you won't," Doc said. "Not ever. The next time you try, the townsfolk will stand against you."

At that moment, Doc Arnold was certain that the Ramsey brothers planned to kill him. The doctor also determined he would say nothing about the information Chance shared with him, about the Indian healing his hand. *Besides*, he thought, *they will all find out soon enough. Let them die learning the truth.*

"I've heard just about enough of your mouth, old man," Duke said, pulling his gun and putting a slug through the doctor's chest.

The doctor slumped over on the floor, a growing pool of blood forming underneath his body.

Cox's face turned a deathly shade of pale. "You killed the doctor, in cold blood," he said. "You promised me you were only going to talk to him."

Duke shrugged. "I reckon we were done talking."

"Come on, Duke," Pete said, his face showing no signs of grief for the kindly old doctor. "We'd better get out of here, just in case someone heard the shot."

"There's nothing to worry about, Pete," Duke said. "If anybody heard the gunshot, they'll just think it was thunder from the storm."

Pete and Duke were laughing about the remark as they went for their horses.

Nearly sick to his stomach over the murder of the doctor, Isaac Cox followed the two brothers into the rainy darkness.

But he wasn't laughing.

* * *

While Chance was trying to sleep that night, he was disturbed by an uneasiness that came to him, an unexplained feeling that death was in the air. The notion continued to bother him for hours, until he finally drifted off to sleep.

Two hours later, he was awakened suddenly, not by a sound, but rather a feeling.

Chance's eyes were instantly alert and he sensed another presence with him and Amy in the room. In the darkness, his hand reached for his gun.

Amy was sleeping soundly, almost dead to the world beside him. Even in the darkness, his eyes could see the entire room clearly. But even though he could feel another presence, nobody was there with them.

Maybe I'm just dreaming, he thought. But just as he decided that it was nothing, little more than a trick of the night, he felt it again.

Looking up, he now saw Yellow Bear was there.

As he moved silently over towards where Chance was sleeping, he motioned at McBride to make no sound. Chance rose up in bed and holstered his gun.

The old Indian's face was pale, but not nearly as tanned and leathery as he remembered. At the same time, the hair of his head was the whitest Chance ever saw.

The Indian moved towards him, with as little sound as a cat sneaking up on his prey. Chance was puzzled by this strange and unexpected appearance.

"This is only for your ears, McBride," Yellow Bear said, barely above a whisper. "I have only a short time. Ask no questions of me."

Chance nodded, saying nothing.

"Twelve men ride against you today. There is much death coming. One has already died."

Forgetting the Indian's admonition, Chance still asked, "Who is dead?"

The Indian looked disgusted.

"I cannot answer you now. You must only listen," Yellow Bear said. "When the riders come, you will not be afraid. Brother Wolf will be at your side and the spirit of the eagle will guide you. You must be strong, McBride. I go now."

Chance rubbed his eyes and the Indian simply disappeared from his sight.

There had been no sound when he left, in much the same way he came. Chance had so many questions to ask him. Who was dead? Who would die? But all of these questions would have to wait until morning.

The manner of Yellow Bear's presence there troubled him. He was sure the Indian hadn't used the door and the window was still down. Chance chuckled to himself, thinking that maybe he shouldn't have drank that beer with Hawkins.

Maybe Yellow Bear was never really here at all.

All his life, Chance never believed in ghosts or apparitions. He always thought they were figments of an overactive imagination. Perhaps he was only dreaming.

With those thoughts still on his mind, Chance drifted back to sleep.

Chapter Fifteen

When the first group of settlers arrived in this valley, they saw it as a fine place for the raising of cattle and horses. The land was good, the soil was fertile, and the harvests would be plenteous.

As they climbed down from their horses and wagons and stared out over the vast horizon, they could not believe their good fortune.

It was beautiful and spacious country, land which was nearly begging for the first plow to be sunk into its rich soil and for an abundance of crops to spring forth from its now-barren womb.

But as those settlers waited on the stragglers, wagons which were delayed and left far behind them because of broken wheels and outbreaks of cholera, they also met the wrath of the Arapaho and the Sioux, who already dwelt in this land.

It was several weeks later and much too late before the stragglers caught up to the first group of settlers.

Glowing faces and a myriad of plans for parties and reunions were crushed by the realization that their friends and fellow travelers had been massacred.

Thinking the Good Lord had led them to this fertile, Western paradise, these tough and weary pilgrims tasted nothing other than Perdition.

Nothing was left of their passing but wind-tossed belongings, blackened boards from the torched wagons, and the scattered bones of the dead.

Along with them, they also found the arrows.

The flesh had been torn from the settlers' bodies by the wolves and ravens, leaving the few bones and skulls which remained to bleach white in the blazing sun.

With women openly weeping, the settlers sorted through the various human bones and damaged skulls, realizing there were other missing and scattered remains of their friends which would never be recovered.

After taking a vote, the settlers decided to bury them where they fell.

The men bent over their shovels, with tears and sweat running down their faces as they dug several individual graves, enough to equal the number of those early travelers who were massacred. Before covering them over and marking their names and years of passing, they tossed at least one bone or skull into each one of the holes.

Instead of planting crops in the soil, the first settlers to arrive in this valley were themselves planted underneath the sod. Their passing was marked by crude, wooden crosses, a gathering of mourners, and soothing words of Scripture.

And on that cloudless but gloomy day, Boot Hill Valley was born in death.

Nobody ever figured on making this place a permanent cemetery. It just sort of happened that way over time, by accident or circumstance.

Later, it only seemed natural to bury those who would die in the years to come next to those who'd gone on before, right there at the head of the valley.

Unmoved by the losses and hardship, these pioneering and hardy souls labored on, transforming this valley into the paradise first envisioned by the dead. Farther down this wide, green valley, the settlers built their homes and farms.

Eventually a town sprang up around them.

Little thought was ever given to what might eventually happen when the harshest rains fell upon the town and upon the graves which dwelt on the same high mountain valley above them.

But on this day, all of those in town would receive another grim reminder.

* * *

Waking from his tortured slumber at the crack of dawn, Chance shaved and got himself dressed. As he put his boots on, he noticed how run-down they were.

If Chance lived through the next couple of days, he reflected morbidly, he knew he would need to buy a new pair. If fate didn't choose to shine on him favorably, then there would be no need.

On this morning, Amy had risen early also. She was already working in the kitchen to prepare him some breakfast.

Chance was pleased to see that the rain let up considerably, as he started out towards the barn to take care of the horses. But from their small place on the far edge of Boot Hill Valley, Chance could still hear the water running down the street.

He feared that if the flooding didn't stop pretty soon, there might not be any town left there to even need a marshal.

One of the older buildings in town had already seen a portion of its foundation washed away and was currently leaning to one side. The owners wouldn't know if the structure could possibly be saved—or was even worth saving—until the flood waters subsided.

Chance quickly took care of his animals and went back inside to enjoy a pleasant breakfast with his wife. The two of them ate silently; they both had secrets.

Amy was fearful of what the day might hold for her husband. Chance was keeping back the story of Yellow Bear's late night appearance in their home.

Slinging the gun belt around his hips, Chance wondered about the vision he saw last night. He wondered if Yellow Bear had really been in his room last night or was he merely dreaming. And even though it seemed so very real to him at the time, he still wasn't sure.

It was clearly hard to deny that the old, Arapaho warrior had some very special abilities, like the times he seemed to instantly know Amy's thoughts and what had happened to the cut he made on Chance's hand. Those were things Chance already knew to be impossible.

After all, how could any man ever really know what a woman was thinking?

Yellow Bear claimed to be an eagle. If that was truly so, Chance wondered if he could be in one place, but also make his spirit appear somewhere else. Or was he just limited to one place at a time?

The more he thought about Yellow Bear, the more curious he became to learn much more about him. Before he went to the office, Chance determined that he would go to the telegraph office and send a wire to the nearest military detachment. Maybe the unit's commander could tell him more about Yellow Bear.

At the same time, Chance knew he might have to concoct a good and convincing story to explain his sudden interest. After all, it wouldn't be wise to go telling a military commander that he, an officer of the law, was in direct contact with a rogue Arapaho warrior, who deliberately fled the governmental-assigned Indian reservation.

Although he might not know for sure whether or not it had been a dream, Yellow Bear, or a figure of the man, warned him that Pete and Duke, along with ten other men, were coming for him today. Perhaps it was only a dream, but still Chance knew he must trust his instincts and prepare for the worst.

For just one brief moment, Chance closed his eyes and pictured the face of Pete Ramsey, the day they left him for dead.

As he saw Pete's face come to his mind, the gun sprang to his hand in barely a heartbeat. Chance knew he was ready, or as ready as he ever would be. And he knew it wasn't only his life or the town he was defending. Amy's safety depended on him.

At that moment, Amy came to him with one last cup of coffee.

"Thanks," he said, taking a sip.

She cringed slightly at the sight of the gun on his hip.

"I wish the killing would stop," Amy said. "I hate it. But most of all, I'm afraid of losing you, Chance. I don't know what I would ever do without you again."

Chance set the cup down on the table and drew her into his arms.

"I'm sure this thing is nearly over, but I don't know how it will all turn out. A lot of people may die before this is all over with. Maybe I'll be one of them. I just don't know."

Amy looked shaken.

"Listen, Amy, I've wasted a lot of my life, drinking and living for the bottle. I'd like to have all that time back, to somehow make it up to you. But I can't," he said, pulling her deeper into his arms. "Before I go to face whatever's out there, there's just one thing I want you to know, Amy. You've always been more woman than any man had the right to deserve in his lifetime. I love you, Amy."

Their lips melted together in a long embrace.

"I've got to go now," Chance said, grabbing his hat. "I should be home to eat around noon."

Amy's eyes followed him to the door. "Chance, please be careful."

He nodded, looked up at the two eagle feathers hanging above the door, and went outside.

* * *

A dozen, well-armed riders, led by Pete and Duke Ramsey, started their horses on the road to a killing. The cavalcade of men, horses, and hardware moved along confidently, defiantly, unlike men expecting to be attacked. Armed as they were, it was unlikely that anyone would seek to hinder them.

Boot Hill Valley was their destination. No mercy was planned for its citizens and no quarter was to be given to them. Two Ramsey kinfolk had been killed and their deaths called for some kind of bloody and final atonement.

The town would be robbed and pillaged as a harsh example of Pete's vengeance. Anyone left alive would be expected to fall into step, taking orders not from the law, but only from the two brothers.

"After we kill McBride," Pete said, "I plan to hang his dead body right in front of the saloon, so that everyone can see what happens to anybody who dares to oppose us."

Following those words, he spat a long stream of tobacco juice from between his greenish teeth. Some of it dribbled down his chin and Pete wiped the remainder off with his shirt sleeve.

"Okay, Pete. What do you want me to do when we get to town," Duke said.

Pete spat again, this time spattering some of the juice on one of the other riders, a man who would have killed almost anyone else who did that to him.

"Go to McBride's house and get his woman. Take Isaac with you, in case you run into any trouble." His teeth bared into a vicious smile. "After her husband is dead, the little woman and I will be wanting to get a little closer acquainted."

Isaac Cox frowned to himself after hearing Pete's plans for the woman. He had no problem with killing a man who had it coming, but harming an innocent woman was something entirely different. And after last night's murder of the doctor, Cox was beginning to have some doubts about the rightness of his actions and the company he was now keeping.

Isaac made no secret of the fact that he had no real love for Chance McBride, or any lawman who tried to dictate what a man could or couldn't do in town. More than once, Cox even considered taking the marshal outside himself, to give him a little dose of another kind of law, the two-fisted kind.

For all his faults, Cox had never done any harm to a lady, a decent lady, like Amy McBride. He struggled with the idea that anybody would even try to make him a party to such a thing. Isaac didn't know what he was going to do. But for now, he thought it best to just say nothing.

"You other men," Pete said, speaking loudly to be heard over the noisy creaks of saddle leather and the steady drum of hoof beats, "do you all know what you're supposed to do?"

Pete continued. "The marshal dies, slow or fast. I don't care. Anyone who stands in our way is to catch a bullet. Is that clear?"

A number of the other riders nodded. Others answered Pete out loud.

"When Chance McBride is face down in that slop hole they call a city street, the town is yours for the taking. Nobody kills my brother and lives to talk about it. I plan to make certain this marshal's luck is just about all run out."

Pete rowelled his horse cruelly. "Come on boys. The town's waiting."

* * *

Although Chance knew water was already flowing down the street the night before, he was in no way prepared for the scene before him now. Torrents of water, nearly two or three feet deep, were crashing through town.

Fortunately, the water level hadn't yet reached the boardwalks, which had been built high above the street.

Boot Hill Valley looked like a town where rows of houses and businesses were foolishly built on each side of a swollen, angry river, with the boardwalks so close to the water a man could fish off of them.

Logs, tree limbs, boards, and other debris were floating down Main Street, carried along by the rushing force of the water. One of the bigger logs failed to make the turn with the current and crashed into the few remaining supports of an older building, which was already leaning sideways after losing half its foundation to the water's earlier erosion.

This latest damage was finally too much for the structure to survive and the building collapsed into the current, the waters pulling much of building's remains down the raging stream.

Farm tools, wagon wheels, even articles of clothing, all of it could be seen, pulled along by the muddy mess of roiling waters.

While still mounted on horseback, Chance saw a couple of dead cats, victims of the flood, go floating right on by him. But even that sight didn't cause McBride nearly as much alarm as what he saw next.

The strength of the raging flood waters lifted a pine casket from its original burial plot. The casket, holding one of the town's more recent victims, was being carried along by the relentless flood. It crashed into the remainder of the fallen structure and burst into splinters, dropping its decomposed corpse into the rushing water, and strewing bones all along its watery path.

Unable to do anything to stop the devastation, Chance merely stared in silence, mouthing a brief word of prayer for the victim's eternal soul.

Looking for a safe place to ford the stream, he waded through to the other side on horseback. Chance climbed down from his saddle and spent several minutes looking for a safe place to tie his horse, where the animal wouldn't be harmed by the floating debris.

He started up the street, slowly, cautiously, all the while expecting the worst. His eyes missed nothing, studying every shadow, alley, door, and window. Few folks were out this time of morning, but each face, feature, and mannerism received his complete attention. Chance knew he must be constantly alert, for his own carelessness might bring about his own death.

His senses, no longer dulled by the effects of the liquor, were sharper than ever, carefully honed to a fine edge. Chance knew this would finally be the day when he must face Pete Ramsey. He could feel it.

If his instincts were correct, he knew he would need eyes in the back of his head. Of course, he had no way of knowing which direction the trouble might come from, so he would need every advantage to survive. He was also counting on an extra big help of just darn good luck.

As he went into the diner, he saw Quentin Rigby Hawkins sitting at a table, putting away a hardy breakfast. He smiled as Chance walked in the door.

"Good morning, marshal," he said. "Please sit down and let me buy your breakfast?"

"Thanks, but I've already eaten. I wouldn't, however, turn down a cup of coffee."

Hawkins called out at the waitress to bring another cup.

Upon bringing the coffee, Chance said, "Thank you very much, ma'am."

Hawkins was sitting on the side of the table, his eyes facing the front of the diner. Chance removed his hat and chose a seat directly against the wall, facing the window, guaranteeing that he would have an unobstructed view of the street.

Hawkins grinned slyly, noting the strange behavior of the marshal in regards to his deliberate choice of seat placement. A student of the West, Hawkins quickly arrived at the reason for his caution. And whatever else he intended to say about it went unsaid.

Chance took a sip of coffee and observed," Hawkins, you hang around like a bad tooth. By the way, thanks for the coffee."

"It was my pleasure, marshal. As I stated before, I owe you a great debt." He paused to sip his coffee. "I fully intend to remain in this town until that debt is sufficiently settled."

"Chance smiled. "It's your funeral, Hawkins. But you better remember one thing. When the bullets start flying, death is not a temporary condition. Anyone can buy a new hat. Heads are a little tougher to replace."

Hawkins reached into his pocket, removing a case. He opened it and produced a couple of cigars, one for each of them.

Chance accepted, bit off the end, and lit it from the match Hawkins was holding. "Thanks again," he said.

After a couple of deep puffs, Chance continued, "Without a wife and children to grieve for you, or carry on your name, your memory lasts just about as long as it takes to shovel in the hole."

"Marshal," Hawkins said, between puffs, "you give the appearance of a typical Western lawman, but your manner of speech betrays you. Strangely enough, you impress me as something of a philosopher. There has obviously been some substantial education in your background, has there not?"

"Education doesn't count for much out here. A man is generally regarded by what he is now, not for something in his past. Yes, Mr. Hawkins, I have had some education, but I try not to let it bother me too much."

Hawkins smiled at the man who sat across the table from him. Meanwhile, the respect these two held for each other continued to grow.

The waitress came and refilled their cups. They sat and talked for several minutes as Hawkins shared tales of England and other faraway lands that Chance had only been fortunate to read about. McBride intently took in every word.

When he finished, Chance spoke of cows, horses, and the vast, God-forsaken land he crossed to get there. Hawkins was a good listener and Chance found himself talking more than was usually his custom.

Just as he stood to leave, a young boy came running into the diner. The youngster, soaked to the skin, was breathing heavily, his brown eyes as large as saucers.

"Marshal," he said, "you'd better come quick!"

"What's the problem, son?"

"It's Doc Arnold. He's been kilt."

For a moment, the boy's message froze Chance in his tracks. For the sake of the town, he quickly pulled himself together and said, "You run on home now, boy. I'll take care of things. One other thing."

"What's that, marshal?"

"Just make sure you don't get carried away by those waters out front."

The boy nodded and obeyed without argument.

As soon as the boy left the diner, Chance muttered underneath his breath, "It's started."

Bursting through the doors of the diner, Chance sprinted all the way to the doctor's office, which was on the same side of the street. Hawkins threw some money down on his table to pay for his meal and went rushing out the door after the marshal.

A crowd was gathered outside the door, each one trying to shove his way forward to view the tragedy inside. Chance elbowed and forced his way through the crowd, with Hawkins right on his heels.

"You people clear out," Chance said. "Go on home."

Although there was some grumbling to be heard, the people began to follow the marshal's orders and started to disperse.

As he entered the room, a grim scene awaited the marshal.

Cursing softly, he knelt beside the body. The aged doctor was dead, a single bullet hole in his chest. The sight of the man, what used to be Doc Arnold, almost made Chance want to retch, right there on the floor. Cold to the touch, Chance figured he must have been murdered late last night.

Hawkins came up beside him. "Was the physician a friend of yours?"

"Yes, he was." Chance said, swallowing hard, "He was a good friend."

"Then my sympathies are truly with you."

Chance nodded. "Thanks, Hawkins."

Then he remembered what Yellow Bear had said to him last night, that one had already died. "So, this is what he meant," he muttered.

Puzzled by the remark, Hawkins stared at him. "What did you say?"

"It was nothing," Chance said. "Doc Arnold was one of the only men in town who dared to speak out against the Ramsey brothers. And it cost him his life."

The undertaker, Douglas Watkins, waited outside the door.

"Douglas, take good care of the man, will you?" Chance said.

"You can count on me, marshal."

"Thank you."

As Chance went out the door and started walking towards his horse, Hawkins continued to follow him."

"You were right about one thing, Marshal."

"What's that?"

"These men are certainly not gentlemen."

Chapter Sixteen

Amy McBride rustled about the kitchen, trying to prepare a delicious meal for her husband. Worried about him as she was, she wanted to do something to lift his burden and also to alleviate her own fears for his life. But cooking dinner was the only thing she could think to do for the man.

The smells of fine cooking escaped the tiny confines of Amy's kitchen, free to be enjoyed by anyone passing near the house. A couple of the locals, who dared to venture outside their house at this time, stopped to delight in the tempting scents coming from the McBride residence.

Intent as she was on the preparation, Amy barely noticed the sound of the door opening. Chance was home early. It brought a smile to her face to see her husband and know that he was safe. She wiped off her hands on her apron and fretted about her appearance.

"Chance," she said, turning towards the door to greet him, "I didn't expect you home yet."

When she saw the face in the doorway, her heart froze in sheer terror.

It was Duke McBride.

Duke was an imposing figure, standing there while filling up the doorway. At the same time, he also cut an impressive figure, with his finest black coat, vest, and string tie. And despite the rain and mud all around them, his boots were still polished to a deep, black shine.

As Amy looked at Duke, she thought that he looked like he'd just come from a wedding or a church service.

"Howdy, ma'am," he said, with a feigned sense of propriety.

Amy did not respond to his seemingly cheerful greeting, knowing that his reason for coming would not be so cordial.

Duke came through the door with Isaac Cox following him.

"Good morning, ma'am," Isaac said, tipping his hat.

Amy's mind was racing, looking for a way of escape.

"What do you want, Mr. Ramsey?" she asked, doing her best to appear calm in spite of her fear.

"I'm just trying to be sociable," Duke said. "Pete and I have been out of town for several weeks, as you already know. Now we're awfully busy, catching up on old acquaintances and such. You know how it is.

"Isaac and I thought we'd just stop by, Mrs. McBride, for a cup of coffee and some small talk." He prodded Cox with an elbow. "Isn't that right, Isaac?"

Cox said nothing.

"You'll get no coffee in my house," Amy said. "I'll not pour coffee for the vermin who shot my husband. Now please state your business and get out."

"Why, that's no way to treat a guest," Duke replied. "Have a seat, Isaac, and the woman will get us some coffee."

The two men pulled back chairs and sat down at the table.

At Duke's suggestion, Amy had a plan come to mind. She remembered there was a rifle in the corner that neither of the men had yet noticed.

Amy filled two cups and carried them over to the table. She gently placed one of them down in front of Isaac, who smiled and nodded. She quickly took the other cup of steaming liquid and tossed it in the face of Duke Ramsey, scalding him severely and temporarily impairing his vision.

Wheeling around, she ran over and grabbed for the rifle. But before she could bring the gun level, a strong arm wrenched the gun from her hands.

"Don't do it, ma'am," Isaac warned. "He'll kill you."

Duke's face, nearly blistered from the hot coffee, rushed over to the woman and grabbed her by the arm, "No, I won't kill her, Isaac," Duke said, "not until Pete's done with you." With that said, he backhanded Amy across the mouth, sending her much smaller body tumbling to the floor.

Just as Duke was pulling back his boot to kick her in the ribs, Isaac Cox stepped between them.

"Don't touch her again!" Isaac demanded, the tone of his voice rising with anger. "Besides, your brother won't care to see her harmed."

Duke saw the determination in the bigger man's eyes and for a moment he stood speechless. "You stay out of this, Cox, or I'll kill you."

In spite of Isaac Cox's enormous size and brawling nature, there was a simple, almost childlike gentleness to the man. It was a characteristic seen by few, most commonly reserved for ladies and small children.

Duke made another effort to step around the big man, but he found his path blocked once more.

Furious that Cox would dare to challenge him, Duke grabbed iron.

Just as Ramsey's gun cleared the holster, a monstrous, rock-hard fist struck him, setting off bells inside his head. And although Duke saw the punch coming his way, the act of drawing his gun left him powerless to prevent it.

The gun fell from Duke's hand as he felt himself falling into a clouded world, filled with confused sounds and images. He hit the floor unconscious, neither feeling nor caring.

Isaac looked at Amy. "He would have killed you, ma'am, just like he did the good doctor."

"The doctor? What are you talking about, Mr. Cox?"

"Last night. Duke murdered Doc Arnold. He shot him down in cold blood."

Her face turned ashen. "How do you know this?"

"I was there, ma'am. But I swear I didn't know he was going to hurt him," Isaac said, the expression on his face revealing the truth in what he was saying.

"My ma taught me right, but I didn't pay her no mind. But no matter how far I've gone astray, I could never let anything happen to a lady, a real lady, like you, I mean."

"No matter what your reasons were, Mr. Cox, I'll never forget what you did to help me. Neither will Chance."

Isaac's gruff yet gentle face turned red, embarrassed by what she said.

"I never liked your husband much, but he was always a man, a good man, much better than any of this bunch. I truly hope he makes it. And once I get you somewhere safe," Isaac said, taking her by the hand, "I plan to go back and help him."

Duke, still stretched out on the floor, was just beginning to stir. His brain had been addled by Cox's right hand and it took a minute for him to regain his senses. As full realization returned to him, he moved slowly, reaching for his fallen gun.

With Isaac and the McBride woman still talking, Duke was certain he could go unnoticed. As his gun came level, he thought, *this will be easy.*

Isaac took hold of the door. "We'd better go, Mrs. McBride, while we still have time to get away."

149

It was then Amy saw Duke raise the gun and a look of fear and shock came to her eyes. "Look out," she warned, the cry coming just a moment too late.

A gun blast exploded in the tiny kitchen.

Isaac Cox never saw Duke fire the shot that took his life. The heavy slug spun him around and he stared, blankly, stupidly, at the gun's smoking, black eye. Cox hit the floor dead.

Scrambling to his feet quickly, Duke pointed the barrel of his gun at Amy's head. "Just give me a reason, woman. Any reason."

Using his foot to kick Cox's body out of the way, Duke pulled up a chair and sat down. His gun was still trained on her. "Have a seat, lady. We'll just wait here. Pete's got to take care of a few loose ends first."

"What do you mean?"

"Don't you play dumb with me. You know I'm talking about your husband," he said, reaching over to take Isaac's cup of coffee. "I might as well drink this, Cox don't look like he'll be needing it."

A cloud of remorse settled upon Amy's soul as she gazed upon the fallen body of Isaac Cox. She knew he died trying to save her. Although Isaac was a hard man, roughly hewn, she had still seen a brave and noble act of kindness in the man. A lonely tear fell from her eye.

Once again, she looked into the empty, cold, and deadly eyes of Duke Ramsey. And for the first time in her life, Amy knew real hatred.

* * *

Chance looked at his watch and saw that it was about twelve o'clock. Amy would have his meal ready, even though he didn't have much of an appetite from seeing Doc Arnold dead.

He checked his gun once again and started for the door, rifle in hand. But just as he was about to open it, a sound outside made him stop with his hand still on the latch.

Dashing over to the window quickly, he peered through the window, but saw nothing outside. Chance knew something was not right. Every instinct was warning him of danger.

It was then he saw it.

A wolf was simply standing in an alleyway across the street. It appeared to stare at him from the distance.

His first thought was that the wolf might have been trapped somehow or driven into town by the flooding. But then Chance remembered the words Yellow Bear said to him last night, about the wolf being with him today.

Like the Indian's visit to him last night, Chance thought this animal's appearance might only be his imagination. Maybe he just didn't get enough sleep. Chance blinked his eyes and looked again, but the wolf was still there.

Once more, the wolf appeared to stare in his direction, seemingly frozen in place. After this pause, the animal turned and went running back up the alley in the other direction.

Chance still didn't know what the Indian meant or how the wolf's presence might make any difference in the battle he must face. But for now, he simply regarded the animal's appearance as a sign, a warning that the battle had come to him and danger now awaited him outside his office door.

An Indian coming into my room at night, a wolf in town looking at me, Chance thought. *I didn't see this many visions when I was drunk.*

Cursing softly, Chance paused by the door. He wanted to draw them out of town, but now, there would be no choice. The battle would happen here.

Taking tight hold of his rifle, Chance jerked the door open and went outside with a roll. If nobody was out there, he knew he might look a little foolish, but that was better than looking a whole lot dead.

As Chance plunged through the door, slugs splintered the boards all around him.

After rolling and coming up on one knee, he fired at the pair of outlaws blazing away at him with their guns.

His first shot took one of them square in the face. Chance levered another couple of shots, one of them missing. The other slug clipped the man's brisket. The would-be killer pitched over on his face in the street, his body carried away by the rushing waters.

At the first sounds of gunfire, the streets of town emptied. Women and children sought cover, as some of the more foolhardy peered outside at the scene through their windows.

Strangely enough, the first sounds of gunfire also signaled an end to three gloomy days of steady rainfall on Boot Hill Valley. The clouds parted and rays of sunlight shone bright on the water's carnage.

As he moved down the boardwalk, Chance tried to stay close to the buildings, deep within their shadows. He hoped it would make him a more difficult target. While under the cover of shadow, he thumbed additional shells into his rifle.

While taking a moment to catch his breath, Chance wondered where Hawkins might be. Although he hadn't seen him since they discovered the doctor's body, he was certain that the Englishman would be somewhere nearby. A body could just about count on it.

Wherever Hawkins might be, Chance was sure that he'd be doing whatever was necessary to help. But he quickly dismissed any thoughts of the Englishman, knowing that he couldn't afford to be distracted by trying to keep both of them alive.

Deciding to move again, he crept across an alley, hunkered down low. As he did, a slug hit the ground right next to his boot, splattering his boots and pants with mud. A buckboard was parked there and Chance flung himself under it.

The man continued firing at him, making it nearly impossible to crawl his way out of the mire. And every time he'd move to the other side of the buckboard, a rifle bullet would cut off any ideas of escape.

As he crouched there, breathing hard, he was busy planning his next move. Sweat trickled down his forehead, making his eyes burn. But with his clothes now covered in mud, he dared not to wipe his eyes.

It was that very moment another thought came to him. He was certain Pete would go after Amy. He was sure of it, a move that was designed to force him out into the open.

Chance knew he would have to get to her first.

* * *

Fully aware what was happening in town, Quentin Rigby Hawkins left the undertaker's office and hurried up to his hotel room. Rummaging through his luggage, he found the brand new revolver he just purchased before making his trip Westward.

It was a fine weapon, he observed. Hawkins removed the box of shells from his bag, loaded all six chambers, and tucked the weapon underneath his belt, hidden by his coat. He also dumped about a couple dozen extra shells in his pockets.

Hawkins was no stranger to a gun, although most of his experience had been at the end of a dueling pistol, defending his honor or that of the ladies. He was also a crack shot, as evidenced by the fact that he was still standing, while two of his challengers hadn't been so fortunate.

Upon returning downstairs, he walked outside on the boardwalk and watched the water carrying away limbs and debris that the flood gathered on its way down the valley.

Looking towards the far end of town, he saw a pair of men loitering on horseback. Generally suspicious by nature, Hawkins didn't believe these were simply a couple of strangers, oblivious to what was happening in town. He was certain that they must be up to something no good.

Making sure to keep himself in the shadows of the buildings, inching his way closer all the time, Hawkins watched them. And when the riders climbed down off their horses, he carefully followed them.

As he peered from the shadows, he saw the men look both ways before going into the house. Their behavior only confirmed his suspicions.

Moving out from under the cover of shadow, he cringed at he walked approached the house. And although eavesdropping had always been distasteful to him, he listened off to the side of the door. Not being able to fully make out what was being said, he slipped around to the window.

From there, he could see everything, the marshal's wife, the two men, and the disagreement that was taking place. Hawkins was shocked when he saw one of the men strike Amy. He was even more alarmed when the bigger man was shot.

He had seen enough.

Moving around to the back door, Hawkins tried the latch and was surprised to discover that the door came open. Once inside, he crept through the house, gun in hand, until he was just outside the kitchen. He stood there and listened.

Since there was no door to the room, he would merely have to enter by stepping through the doorway.

From the sounds of the conversation, Hawkins surmised that the man inside was Duke Ramsey and that could only mean that the marshal's wife was in grave danger.

Quietly, Hawkins checked his gun and eared back the hammer of his revolver. Gathering his courage, he decided the time must be now . . .

Chapter Seventeen

As Duke Ramsey waited for his brother, Pete, Amy sat there at the kitchen table, with the body of Isaac Cox dead at their feet.

Uncertain of what to do, but knowing he must do something to save her, Hawkins waited outside the kitchen, his mind working to come up with some kind of distraction.

It was then the first sounds of gunfire broke the silence.

"You hear those shots, lady," Duke said. "Now you're a widow."

Upon hearing the gunfire and certain that he would get no better distraction, Hawkins sprang into the room.

Upon seeing the man, Duke jumped up from his chair, clawing for his gun. Amy hit the floor, searching for her rifle.

In his haste to save the woman, Hawkins fired much too quickly and his first shot missed. By that time, Ramsey's gun was spitting flame.

The Englishman felt a burning pain, a slug knocking the already-damaged bowler hat from his head. A sudden sense of lightheadedness immediately swept over him, but he remained upright. Boldly Hawkins stood his ground and returned fire, as his next shot grazed Duke's cheekbone.

Duke swore loudly as hot lead seared his face.

The room was filled with a cloud of gunsmoke, making it increasingly difficult for anyone to find a clear target. Unable to locate her rifle, Amy ignored the blood and wrenched the six-gun from the dead man's holster. She cocked the weapon and brought it up to fire.

Duke, sensing that he no longer had any control of the situation, saw no reason to die just to satisfy his brother's carnal desires. He sprinted out the door just as Hawkins and Amy fired simultaneously.

Their twin bursts of gunfire exploded the door jamb, just behind the fleeing outlaw.

"Bloody hell. He got away." Hawkins said, quickly apologizing to the woman for his slip of the tongue.

"That's quite all right, Mr. Hawkins. At this moment, I feel much the same way," she said, throwing him a smile. "Thank you so much. I don't know what would have happened to me if you hadn't helped."

"It was my pleasure," Mrs. McBride," Hawkins said, with one hand pressed against the side of his head. Blood began dripping between his fingers.

Upon seeing the blood, Amy rushed to his side. "You'd better sit down, Mr. Hawkins. You've been shot"

"No, thank you, ma'am," he replied, holding his gun and staggering towards the door. "It is only a small wound to the flesh. And I must go to help the marshal."

Seeing the man struggle to walk, Amy grew more insistent.

"Please sit down, Mr. Hawkins."

I should be fine," he replied before collapsing onto the floor.

Amy grabbed a towel from the kitchen, knelt down on the floor, and began to care for the unconscious Englishman.

As she began to dab the blood away from his wound, Amy said, "You, Mr. Hawkins, are just about as stubborn and mule-headed as someone else I know."

* * *

Knowing he needed to get to Amy, Chance's next move was a foolhardy one. He darted his head out from underneath the wagon, just long enough to lever a shot at the man on the far roof and took off running down the boardwalk.

Running for his life, covered with mud, legs churning, lungs bursting, bullets were striking boards all around the base of his heels. Another gunman appeared from between the buildings, jumping right in front of him.

Having no time to shoot, Chance swung the barrel of his rifle against the man's head, loosing the outlaw's gun from his hand and sending him tumbling into the stream.

Chance saw the man go into the water, but heard nothing more than the man's screams as the water claimed another victim.

All at once, Chance saw another disturbing sight, one which instantly gave him a sense of hope. Another couple of caskets, still undamaged by the current came floating in his direction.

Unable to continue evading the gunfire of the man on the roof and seeing another couple armed men in his path, he took the only route of escape available to him.

Taking a firm hold of his rifle, Chance ran to the edge of the boardwalk, and cast himself into the murky, cold, and raging waters. Slugs hitting the water all around him, he managed to grasp hold onto one of the caskets.

The water was icy cold and it felt like a million little daggers were plunging into his flesh. Clinging to the Grim Reaper's hope chest, while holding his head just barely above the surface of the water, the box shielded him from the rifleman above.

The floating coffin carried him along until it came alongside the fallen building. Taking a huge risk, Chance let go of the casket and desperately grasped for one of the boards of the fallen building.

Grasping the board with one hand and holding the stock of the rifle in the other, it took nearly every bit of strength he had to somehow pull himself free of the chilly, raging water's grip.

Upon leaving the water and climbing back onto the boardwalk, the marshal was once more in clear view of the rifleman from across the street. Ramsey's ranch hand drew a bead and squeezed the trigger, hearing nothing but a metallic click.

His rifle was now empty.

But Chance's was still loaded.

Throwing the gun to his shoulder, Chance never gave him the slightest opportunity to duck under cover. He levered a quick shot into Ramsey's ranch hand, mortally wounding the outlaw and sending him sprawling from the roof into the cold, dark waters below.

Soaking wet and shivering from the cold, Chance once more started racing down the boardwalk, praying he could reach his wife in time.

As he dashed along the row of storefronts, another outlaw, hiding inside one of them, snapped off a shot at Chance through the window glass. The slug would have scored had it not hit the gun instead.

The blast shattered the stock of McBride's rifle.

Chance threw down the now-useless gun and took a quick glance at his holster, to make sure his six-gun survived the swim. Seeing it was still there, he palmed the gun and stepped to the side of the shattered window glass.

Chance leaned in and began firing at the man hiding inside. His three shots barely missed the fleeing outlaw as he scrambled out the back of the store.

Knowing that he made to easy a target in the sunlight, Chance once again stepped in the shadows, long enough to eject the empty shells and replace them.

The outlaw, who just ran out the back of the store, came around the next building and saw the marshal step into the darkness. Seeing another opportunity to kill McBride, he crept silently along the face of the building. He knew the marshal hadn't yet detected his presence behind him.

McBride was still thumbing shells into his gun when he raised the rifle and pointed it at the marshal's back. As his finger began tensing on the trigger, a cruel smile came to his lean, unshaven face.

Although he heard movement, Ramsey's man seemed to sense the presence of something behind him.

Upon turning around, he was being stalked by a lone and hungry wolf, its long and deadly teeth bared and snarling.

He swung his rifle around to kill it, but the vicious animal was already leaping through the air at the man. The outlaw would see nothing more than sharp and angry claws and teeth.

The determined predator pounced upon the frightened ranch hand, its teeth ripping and tearing at his throat. The bloody man cried out in pain, but only for a moment, as the wolf's strong jaws crushed out any of his further cries for help.

At the sound of this latest noise, Chance wheeled around, gun at the ready. But upon seeing the wolf, he could see that the animal had already eliminated the threat. And it was clear he could do absolutely nothing to help the man.

The wolf, his fangs dripping blood, stood there staring at Chance. And under normal circumstances, the events that just transpired behind him would have instilled a fear that the creature would attack Chance also.

But on this day, the marshal had no fear of the wolf.

And with everything that had already happened to him, Chance was actually starting to believe these strange and incredible tales of his friend, the old Arapaho warrior.

Knowing that he owed his life to this predator's attack and pleased to still be alive, Chance holstered his gun.

The wolf paused and looked into his eyes once more, as though two tough but respected adversaries were facing one another on the battle-field, opponents who each decided they would rain no harm upon the other.

Then the two of them each turned to go on their separate ways.

As he slogged through the mire of the alley, Chance began to climb back up the boardwalk and came face to face with Willie Pickett and Jim Crosby, the pair of Pete's men who blocked his path earlier. Chance knew he would have no more luck in getting around them.

They could only be confronted.

These were tough men, ones with all the bark still on them. Both of them had the reputation as good cowhands, more than worthy of the monthly pay they drew. Although they were no strangers to the gun, each of them was much better with a rope or working from the saddle.

"You men are much too good to be running with this outfit and I don't think they'll be anybody left to pay you before this day's over," Chance said. "Besides, I don't want to kill you boys."

"You're going to have to, marshal," Jim said. "I ride for the brand."

"That goes double for me," Willie added.

"I'm only going to ask you men one more time. Step aside."

Chance's eyes watched them, conscious of their every breath.

"There ain't no shame in throwing in your cards when you know the deck's stacked against you," Chance said. "I'll get at least one of you. Maybe both. Like I said already, Pete will be dead before sun-down, so you men don't ride for him anymore."

"Who're you trying to kid?" Willie said. "Ramsey told us you can't even use a shootin' iron."

"I guess one or both of you will have to die to find out." Chance watched their eyes, his hand only inches away from the butt of his gun. "Which will it be? A fast draw or a fast horse? Make up your minds."

For a brief moment, Chance was certain they were going for their guns. In fact, Jim was a proud man, who already decided to draw on the marshal, but Willie's voice stopped him.

"I hear Montana is nice this time of year."

Jim relaxed and coaxed a smile. "Probably needing a couple of good cowhands up that way, I reckon."

"Probably so," Willie added. "We've ridden a lot of trails together, ain't we, Jim? I'd be obliged to see a few more."

Willie started to unbuckle his gunbelt.

"Keep your guns, boys," Chance said, with a smile. "Montana's some rough country."

"Good luck to you, marshal," Jim said, tipping his hat. "Guess Pete and Duke were all wrong about you."

With a sigh of relief, Chance smiled when he saw Pickett and Crosby turn around and head for their horses. When he was certain the two of them weren't about to change their minds, he could think of nothing other than protecting Amy.

Stepping inside the alley where he tied his horse, Chance found himself staring into the soulless eyes of Pete Ramsey.

"Afternoon, Pete," Chance said.

"Afternoon, marshal."

"By the way, Pete, you're under arrest."

Two other armed men came up behind Chance. He heard them when they eared back the hammers on their revolvers.

Now they have me, Chance thought.

Even if Chance was fast enough to outdraw Pete, the others would shoot him down, right where he stood. *It doesn't matter*, Chance thought. *I'm going to kill Pete, for Amy's sake.*

No matter the outcome, Chance decided to do whatever must be done.

Pete's tobacco-stained, green teeth greeted Chance with an evil smile. Leaning his shoulder on the side of the building, his makings were out and he was calmly rolling a cigarette. When he finished, Pete struck a match on the side of the building and lit up. After taking a couple of puffs, he resumed talking.

"You done right fine for a man only having one good hand."

Chapter Eighteen

Most folks give little daily thought to law and order, or its necessary and rightful place in a civilized society.

When the West was still wild and untamed, the only law that existed was that which a man could enforce at his own hand. With the coming of settlers and businesses, churches and schools, and most importantly, the increasing influx of women, men were routinely hired by the townspeople to enforce the law in their stead.

Most individuals call this civilization, and they heartily welcome and embrace its arrival.

But all too often, civilization leads to weakness and apathy on the part of its people. Men often become unwilling to lift a finger in the defense of another. Although some are just uncaring, most are simply unwilling to suffer the consequences and are content to let someone else pay the price for the safety of those around them.

This condition often changes when a person's own home is touched or his treasured manner of living is somehow threatened. When faced with riots and anarchy, public-minded citizens will eventually lend a hand to the rightful authorities or bear a weapon themselves for the reestablishment of law and order.

The people of Boot Hill Valley had finally reached this point of dissatisfaction.

Until today, the situation in town had been seen as a personal blood-feud between a couple of unflinching adversaries, a matter which could only be settled by Pete Ramsey and Marshal Chance McBride.

But all of that changed with the cold-blooded murder of Doc Arnold.

The kindly, old doctor's death galvanized an entire community, which quickly declared war against the lawless element in town.

And then there were the three innocent citizens who died this day from the guns of Ramsey's men; all of it was too much for the citizens to stand anymore.

Taking up rifles and revolvers, normally peaceful citizens, driven to action, moved down the boardwalks in a massive show of force.

Like a battalion of soldiers, they stormed upon the place where Chance McBride and Pete Ramsey faced one another. Then they leveled guns on the outlaws behind the marshal.

Something in Pete's eyes changed when he saw himself facing a lawman, who was now backed by dozens of storekeepers and townspeople, all of them holding weapons. Some of the swagger went out of him, but his face still held a smile.

Douglas Watkins, the local undertaker, said, "Marshal, it's your call. We'll do whatever you say."

"Yeah, if you want to settle it here," Sam Howard replied, "we'll keep the dogs off of you. Either way, Pete Ramsey's harmed his last person in Boot Hill Valley."

"Thanks," Chance said. "It's right comforting to know that someone is covering your back."

He returned his attention towards Pete. "This is between you and me. But I'm giving you this one chance to turn yourself in."

Pete Ramsey might be evil, but he was clearly not stupid. Until this time, he had successfully intimidated the people of the town into submission. Although his skills with a gun were good enough to take most any one of them in a one-on-one fight, Pete also knew he was no match for an armed and angry crowd.

Even if he killed the marshal, one of them would eventually put a bullet in him. And if the bullet didn't kill him, the outraged townspeople probably wouldn't even wait for a trial and would simply string him up before the sun fell.

Pete just smiled as an evil gleam shone in his eye. "What difference does it make? You're just going to hang me anyway."

At that moment, the crowd, sensing that something was about to happen, began to step back from the line of fire.

"Maybe so," Chance said, "but I promise you'll get a fair trial. That's a lot more than you and your brother gave Doc Arnold."

"That's a fine looking woman you're married to, McBride. She's too damn young to be a widow. These people will get me, I'm sure, but you'll still be dead. Why don't you drop this while you still have a chance?"

"You know I can't do that, Pete."

Ramsey's eyes turned cold as he flicked his cigarette away. "Can't or won't?"

"It's all the same thing. I'm the marshal here."

Pete laughed out loud. "The law you say. I make my own law, marshal."

"This is your last chance, Pete. Drop your gun. Now."

"You killed Jason, McBride. I can't let you get away with that. I can't . . ."

Pete's hand flashed for his gun.

Many of those standing around that day later testified that they never saw the marshal draw his weapon. But they all saw the smoking gun in his hand as it was firing.

Pete's gun cleared the holster and something burned Chance's arm.

But Chance triggered his gun, again and again, knowing that he must bring Ramsey down.

Pete continued firing, eyes blazing, standing there like a sturdy, old oak tree. His second shot hit nothing, passing harmlessly between Chance's body and his firing arm. The last one was fired wildly, sending hot lead through the lung of one his hired hands, who hit the ground only a few brief moments from death.

Chance squeezed off the last shot and saw the gun fall from Pete's weakened fingers. But despite the wounds he suffered, the man continued to remain upright.

Had it not been for the pair of crimson stains on his chest, Chance might have thought he missed.

But he hadn't missed.

Pete Ramsey was dead. He just didn't know it yet.

Ramsey began walking towards him. "There's no way you can beat me, McBride," he said, starting to sway on his feet. "How did you do it?"

As he reholstered his gun, Chance just looked at Pete. "You wouldn't believe me if I told you."

It was the last thing Pete ever heard as he toppled over on his face.

Pete Ramsey was dead.

It was a fitting outcome to an otherwise worthless life, a violent man fallen in a violent manner. Like so many of his kind, those before and those to come later, a bullet waited at the end of life's journey.

His had been a bloody path, littered with the bodies of honest lawmen and innocent citizens, people deserving of a much better fate. Ramsey's death did not pay for his crimes, the broken dreams of his victims, or the blood that was shed by his hand.

Judgment for those would be issued by a Higher Court, a Supreme Judge who could not be swayed by power or money.

As much as he thought he should, Chance could not grieve for the soul that lay at his feet. That fact bothered him some.

During his quest to bring Pete Ramsey to justice, a part of himself had been lost, something precious, a quality which he could never get back.

Everyone in Boot Hill Valley, they had all lost something.

People began to filter out of their houses and storefronts, joyously gathering around them. Unburdened by a fear that often consumed them, the people were ready to celebrate their newfound freedom.

Rifle in hand, Amy came running toward Chance, pushing her way through the crowd. She dropped her gun and threw herself into his outstretched and waiting arms.

"Chance," she said, "I'm so glad you weren't hurt."

His lips melted with hers. "Not much, I wasn't."

Then she saw the blood dripping from his wounded arm. "You've been shot."

"It ain't nothing, Amy. Barely a scratch."

"You just hush your mouth, Chance McBride," Amy replied. "You're the second stupid man who's told me that today."

All around him, Chance could hear snickers.

"All right, you folks," Chance said, "the show's all over for today. Let's get these bodies out of the street."

A number of those in the crowd began to drift away to their various homes and duties. Others stopped to carry away the bodies of the fallen.

Amy bent down and tore away at the hem from her skirt, using it for a make-shift bandage to wrap Chance's arm.

As she was nursing her husband's minor wound, Hawkins joined them there, his head still bandaged. The butt of a revolver was sticking out from under his belt.

"It looks like you did not come out of this totally unscathed, marshal," Hawkins said, with an ever-widening smile across his face.

"I sure look a whole lot better than you do," Chance said, returning his smile. "And I could have sworn I told you to keep your head down, Hawkins."

At the moment, he saw no real humor in the statement.

"Duke had taken me hostage," Amy explained. "Mr. Hawkins came to my aid and shot it out with him. He saved my life, Chance."

"A lot of good it did," Hawkins added, dryly. "He escaped anyway."

Chance walked over and shook his hand. "Thank you anyway, Hawkins. Now, I'm in *your* debt."

He nodded.

"Duke was the one who murdered Doc Arnold," Amy said. "Isaac Cox told me so, right before Duke killed him too."

One of the spectators located Chance's hat and returned it to him, something he lost in the earliest moments of the gun battle. The marshal returned the hat to his head. Another citizen came towards them, leading the marshal's horse.

"You know I'll have to go after him, don't you, Amy?"

Her eyes softened. "I know you do, Chance. Please be careful."

Chance nodded.

"I'll ride along with you," Hawkins said.

"No, you won't, Hawkins. I need you here."

The Englishman looked puzzled.

"How would you like to be my deputy?"

"I would be proud to do so," he shot back, the gleam in his eye returning.

Chance threw his arm around the Englishman's shoulder and walked him out of earshot of the now-dwindling crowd. He whispered so as not be heard.

"Some of these people are mighty bitter about the death of Doc Arnold," Chance said. "They're likely to string up the rest of Pete's outfit, just for good measure. Some innocent men could get their necks stretched, just for being in the wrong place at the wrong time."

Hawkins listened carefully, saying nothing.

"You're a good man, Hawkins. I need you to see that these men live long enough to get a fair trial. Do you think you're up to the job?"

"Yes, sir, marshal. You can count on me."

"Well, I reckon I'd better swear you in. Raise your right hand."

Hawkins raised his hand.

"Quentin Rigby Hawkins, do you solemnly swear to uphold all the laws of the town of Boot Hill Valley, of the great state of Colorado? If so, please say, 'I do.'"

"I do," repeated the Englishman.

"Congratulations, Mr. Hawkins. You are now a Colorado deputy marshal," he said, temporarily removing the badge from his vest. "Wear this one until I get another. And now you're taking orders from me.

"Make sure all of the remaining Ramsey men get safely behind the bars of the jail. You can get Sam Howard to help you. I don't believe in mob justice. So, whatever happens, don't give any of them over to a crowd."

"Yes, sir, marshal."

"And if you have any trouble with the crowd, get one of the shotguns out of the rack in my office. Shotguns speak louder to a mob."

He nodded. "I won't let you down, marshal."

Chance smiled. "I never once thought you would. And one more thing, Hawkins."

"What would that be?"

"Go buy yourself a decent hat."

Chance took the reins away from the young man who was holding his horse. He thanked him and led his horse over to where Amy was standing. Her eyes showed a host of worry that her lips refused to speak.

His arm slipped around her waist and he bent down to firmly kiss her soft lips.

"I'll be back soon, Amy," he said, swinging into the saddle and leaning his forearm on the saddlehorn.

"You'd better come back, Chance McBride."

Chance reined his horse around and galloped out of town.

Chapter Nineteen

Duke Ramsey, having lost his urgent need for vengeance, straddled a horse and was headed southward, bound for parts still unknown. Nearly being killed by the Englishman and a woman was more than enough to instill in him a real hankering for travel.

After fleeing the woman's house, he'd lingered just long enough to get the scent of what was happening in Boot Hill Valley. He watched the armed mob of citizens go charging down the street. Duke was pretty sure his surviving ranch hands and gunmen were now in jail. Everything that remained behind was now lost to him.

His brother's personal battles were no longer something worth dying for; they never were.

Over the years, Duke heard many stories about what vigilantes in a town like this often did to those who fueled their rage. His brother, Pete, was on his own now.

Most likely, Pete was already dead. If not, he soon would be.

With his uncle and his brothers dead, Duke knew he had nobody else to worry about except himself.

Duke certainly had no desire to stay around for the coming necktie party. And the death of the doctor was certain to get him hanged, since the woman and the Englishman already knew he was responsible.

He was simply an outlaw on the run, soon to have a price on his head.

Following the days of rain, the sun was now relentless in the Colorado sky. Once again, he stopped his horse long enough to take another long pull from his canteen. Duke could feel the contents of his canteen dwindling. He wished he'd thought far enough ahead to steal one before he left town. He would need to replenish his water supply soon.

An eagle cried out above him, searching for its prey.

As Duke looked above, he pushed back his hat and scratched his head. He thought the eagle was flying unusually low in the sky. Then he laughed to himself.

At least it isn't a buzzard circling my dead hide.

Duke knew his best chance for survival was to cross into Arizona Territory. From there, he could find another comfortable place to hang his hat. Perhaps he could even slip into Mexico if the pressure from the law became too strong.

He shook out the reins and continued riding.

Duke remembered a place not too far from there where he could refill his canteen. And after all the rain they had lately, it was certain to have an abundant supply of water.

As for McBride, the marshal would always be there and Duke was certain there would be another time for them to meet. And if the opportunity presented itself, he determined the woman and the Englishman would get theirs too.

Duke smiled to himself. At least he wouldn't go hungry.

His saddlebags were stuffed full of Ramsey money, the proceeds of their cattle drive and the rest of their operating cash, removed from the family safe before they left. At the time, he figured it was wise to be prepared, if the worst were somehow to happen.

Even Pete didn't know he took the money before they left.

Pete always was a fool.

Stopping to check his back trail, Duke was certain he saw a small cloud of dust off in the distance.

It looked like a single rider, maybe an hour behind him.

Duke smiled. Maybe he wouldn't have to wait all that long to kill the marshal. And then he thought of it.

McBride will need water too.

While Duke's horse continued to move on down the trail, his mind was working on a plan

After refilling his own canteen at the watering hole, maybe he would just hide out there and wait for the marshal to arrive. Duke decided that he would find a comfortable spot to sit, grab his Winchester and some jerked beef from his saddlebags, and just get comfortable to wait a spell.

The watering hole was a real good place for an ambush.

After he dry gulched McBride, it wouldn't only give him a spare canteen, it would also provide him with a spare horse.

The longer Duke rode, the better the idea sounded to him.

Almost two hours later, Duke saw the watering hole just ahead of him. His canteen long since empty, he smiled through lips which were now growing parched and brittle.

But Duke was confident there was water just ahead of him, because his horse already smelled it a while earlier. For the past few minutes, he'd been holding back on the reins, keeping the horse from breaking into a run.

From behind an outcropping of rocks near the watering hole, a pair of dark eyes studied the weary rider who was now approaching. The one who spied Duke Ramsey had nowhere to go, nothing to do. He had nothing but time, time to sit, to watch, and to wait.

Knowing that the Whites needed water more often than his people, the Indian had simply determined which way the man was traveling and rode on ahead. The Great Spirit led him here. The Arapaho smiled, knowing that the one he waited on was coming.

Still holding tight to the reins with his left hand, Duke removed his hat, wiping his brow with his right shirt sleeve, before returning the hat to his head. The afternoon sun was relentless. And after stopping to check a couple of times, he knew the marshal was closely on his trail.

But now that he arrived here, Duke knew his worries would soon be forgotten.

Sweet, cool water awaited him on the other side of this rocky outcropping. As he reined his horse through the rocks, his mind was on nothing but the water ahead.

At that moment, Duke felt a sudden, added burden stagger his horse, as something, or someone, leaped upon them from a rock above.

Before Duke's thirst-driven and weary mind could fully grasp what was happening, a wiry, muscular arm locked around his throat. Strong as Duke was, he struggled to catch a breath. The unexpected attack left him unable to escape the steely, trap-like grasp around his neck.

It was then Duke saw the knife come around in front of his body, poised for a killing blow, the blade glistening brightly in the blazing, afternoon sun.

Realization came swiftly and Duke reached out to stop the knife-wielding arm, a moment too late.

Duke heard a dull, sickening thud, as the sharp blade of the Indian pierced his ribcage. A sharp, scorching pain startled him and Duke's confused, dying mind tried to understand the reason for his discomfort. He looked down and was disgusted to see blood flowing on the front of his finest, white shirt.

Despite the Indian removing the arm from around his throat and dismounting, Duke's breathing was still growing labored and more difficult. His parched lips were now moist. He touched them and wiped away blood.

This can't be happening, he thought. *I had a plan.*

It was then Duke decided his cinch must be coming loose, because he felt himself falling. Falling.

Duke tumbled from his saddle, falling onto the rocky ground.

A tugging at his gunbelt awakened him. Duke's confused and bleary eyes opened to find an old, weather-hardened, red face staring down at him.

The Arapaho said nothing, as he admired the man's well-polished boots and fine clothes. Having no real use for them, the Indian removed Duke's gunbelt and led away his horse.

The Indian made no effort to finish Duke off, for the man's death was inevitable, slow and painful, but sure as the sun.

Ramsey tried to call out, but words would not come. The Indian rode away. A couple of moments later, he saw what appeared to be an eagle, landing on the rocks above him.

Its keen and knowing gaze seemed to be fixed upon him.

He always wondered what death would be like. His clouded, scarcely-open eyes searched for the angels, but there would be none for Duke.

His throat dry as the sifting sand, Duke licked his lips, which now tasted like salty iron. Once more remembering the waterhole, he struggled to rise. His effort was useless. Duke trembled violently for a moment and then lay still.

The eagle lifted from his rocky perch, spreading his vast wings as he glided through the air, flying over to Ramsey's fallen body.

The eagle lighted upon Duke's chest, peered over its beak into the man's unseeing eyes, and then lifted for its rightful place in the skies, soaring among the clouds.

Chapter Twenty

After riding out of Boot Hill Valley, Chance picked up Duke's trail with no real effort. And since he made no great effort to hide it, Chance rode along carefully, ever wary of being taken in a trap.

After surviving everything that happened to him in town earlier, Chance knew if he got himself killed now, Amy would never let him rest in peace.

If possible, Chance wanted to bring the doctor's murderer back to town alive. He desperately wanted Duke to stand trial. Although he knew it was likely Duke wouldn't escape the gallows, Chance still figured there had already been enough killings for one day.

Like Duke Ramsey, Chance also knew about the distant watering hole and figured that must be where the outlaw was headed. He wiped the sweat from his brow and took a long drink from his canteen.

Chance was especially pleased the kid in town who brought him his horse had thought enough to provide him a second, full canteen. He was always impressed by the rare, forward thinking of any young man.

It was an outstanding quality in a kid.

In anyone.

Several hours later, Chance palmed his gun and rode wide circles around the waterhole, mindful of every sight and sound around him. He stopped only long enough to climb down and study the tracks of a single horse, moving away from the water.

The animal was being ridden. And whoever was riding it was riding away the horse on which Duke had been mounted.

Chance removed his hat and scratched his head. He took another drink of water and puzzled over the scene for a time.

Forking his saddle once again, Chance continued riding smaller circles around the watering hole, until he was convinced nobody was lying wait to ambush him.

It was then he saw the body upon the ground.

Even from a distance, the style of the fallen man's fine dress revealed his identity to anyone who knew him.

Still leery of a trap, Chance kept one fist full of iron as he slowly eased his horse through the rocks. Staring down at the body on the ground, there was no doubt that Duke had been dead for some time.

His body rested next to the waterhole, peaceful and unmoving, the shiny toes of his boots pointed skyward. The wind was picking up and it filtered dust from the rocks all over the dead man's frame.

Chance holstered his gun, dismounted, and dropped the reins, allowing his thirsty horse to run ahead to the water's edge.

As he studied the tracks and the signs, it was obvious what happened there.

Someone had been lurking among the rocks, waiting there for a potential victim. When the rider approached, the attacker took him by surprise, leaping upon the back of his horse and stabbing Duke in the chest.

Chance was sure it must have been an Indian, because there were moccasin tracks among the rocks and all around the body. Duke's gunbelt had been taken, along with the horse, whose tracks he studied earlier.

Not having a second horse on which to return the body, Chance decided to bury the body not too far from the water. Duke would have his own little Boot Hill right among the rocks, next to the small mesquite which grew there.

Chance figured Duke Ramsey would finally do the first worthwhile act he ever performed, his dead body giving nourishment to another living thing.

After stripping off his shirt, he found a sharp rock and began scraping out a hole.

A little over an hour later, Chance wiped the sweat from his body with his shirt, took another long drink of water, and walked over to get the body for burial.

While standing over the body, Chance now saw something which sent chills all through his body.

In spite of all his study, Chance had somehow failed to see it before.

Clutched inside Duke's dead hand was a single eagle's feather.

* * *

Four days later, the water had receded from the streets of Boot Hill Valley and life was finally returning to normal.

But this was a much better kind of normal, one in which its now much happier citizens no longer felt threatened by the Ramsey brothers on a daily basis.

The townsfolk were working hard and actively rebuilding those things which were destroyed by the raging flood waters.

Although there was still plenty of mire on its main street, the coffins and bones which had been strewn along by the flood had been collected by the undertaker and were waiting a return to the ground, hopefully for their last and final, eternal rest.

The town had even voted to relocate the cemetery and would start the long and arduous process of digging up those graves which were undisturbed by the flood waters and reburying them in their new location.

The town's newest Boot Hill would finally be stationed in a location undisturbed by future ravages of nature.

Leaning back in a chair against the front of the jail, his foot resting on the rail out front, Hawkins polished his new badge while he watched all the work taking place in town. Jumping up when he saw the marshal approach, the Englishman returned the shiny badge to its place on front of his coat.

"Relax, Hawkins. Sit back down," Chance said, taking his place in a chair right beside him. "How are the prisoners?"

"They are well, sir," Hawkins replied. "The lady just brought their food down from the diner. They are eating now."

"Good," Chance said. "I just got a telegram from Denver. The U.S. Marshal should be arriving by this time tomorrow to take them off our hands."

Hawkins smiled. "For that outcome, I am most pleased. I am growing weary of caring for this rabble."

"Me too. How's your head?"

"It's feeling much better now. I scarcely even remember the injury occurred," Hawkins said. "Thank you for your concern."

Chance grinned at his new deputy. "Had to go and buy yourself another ugly hat, didn't you?"

"Whatever do you mean?" Hawkins said, removing the hat from his head and dusting it off with his elbow. Satisfied with its appearance, the Englishman returned the bowler to his head. "This is the same type of hat worn by Bartholomew Masterson, a famed Western hero, known as Bat by many of you Yanks."

"You might want to study Bat Masterson's life a little more closely," Chance said. "Even he was smart enough to know a stupid hat won't protect you from a bullet. If you want to live as long as Masterson, you might want to keep your head down in the future. And there's one other thing."

"What is that, marshal?"

"I suggest you use that word, *Yanks*, sparingly. A number of these good people took up arms for the Confederacy. They wouldn't take kindly to you, or anyone else, referring to them by that term."

"I will keep that in mind, sir."

"You'll live much longer if you do."

"It's about time I made my rounds." Chance rose from his seat. "Come with me, Hawkins. With me back in town, those boys inside will be fine until we get back."

The two of them started up the street, passing in front of the stores and shops, pausing occasionally to speak to someone or to exchange a greeting.

"I never got an opportunity to thank you, Hawkins, for the fine work you did in protecting those prisoners. Sam Howard told me about it. Bragged on you a lot."

Their paths crossed with a woman headed the other way on the boardwalk and they each briefly tipped their hats to her.

"I must admit I was frightened when it happened. But it was just like you suggested, marshal. I suppose a number of them lingered too long at the ale that evening."

"It probably wasn't just the ale that was fueling them."

"Whatever spirits they were consuming, I certainly had some anxious moments," Hawkins said, his eyes twinkling. "You were certainly correct, sir. I do have to admit that a single blast from that shotgun has a sobering impact on those around it."

"Yes, it does. But not a lot of men would still have the grit to face down a mob like you did, Hawkins. From what I've seen, you should make one hell of a good, Western lawman."

The two of them continued walking, crossing over the still-muddy street, and walking back on the other side.

"Have you heard from your friend, Yellow Bear?"

Since giving him the job as his deputy, Chance believed the Englishman had a right to know everything. One afternoon, they sat down over dinner and he shared with Hawkins the story of his experiences with the Indian.

The Englishman listened in uncomfortable silence, leaving Chance uncertain of how much, if any, Hawkins believed of his story.

He couldn't blame the deputy if he remained at all doubtful. Even after seeing it himself, Chance still struggled to accept it all.

"Haven't seen hide nor hair of him. Not sure if I ever will again."

Before the two men returned to the jail, after finishing their rounds, a small company of military soldiers rode into town. The blue uniforms were resplendent in the bright, cloudless rays of Colorado sunlight.

Upon seeing the badges, the blue-coated riders rode up the street to where the pair stood. The one in front, a major, lifted his gloved hand, clearly a signal for the other soldiers with him to draw rein.

"I am Major Jeremy Witlow of the U.S. Army. Would either of you men happen to be Marshal Chance McBride?"

"Pleased to meet you, Major," Chance said. "I'm McBride."

While the others waited, the major climbed down from his horse and looking up at one of the others, he said, "Sergeant, go on down to the saloon and get you and these good men a beer. One beer. Is that understood?"

The sergeant saluted. "Quite clear, sir. Will you be joining us?"

"Yes, sergeant. Give me just a minute with Mr. McBride."

"Yes, sir," he responded, starting his horse down the street, followed closely by the others.

Major Witlow walked up the stairs toward them and they all briefly shook hands, as Chance introduced his deputy.

"What can I do for you, Major?"

"Do you have a moment to talk?"

"Yes, I do, Major."

Sensing that the discussion might be a private matter, Hawkins excused himself and went back over to check on the prisoners.

"Good day, Major," Hawkins said.

"Good day to you as well, Deputy Hawkins."

"I understand you recently sent us a telegram, asking about a renegade Arapaho, named Yellow Bear. Is that correct?"

"Yes, it is."

"May I inquire as to your interest in this matter?"

"A couple of the locals have reported thefts of cattle and horses. A few of them suspected that it might be the work of Yellow Bear."

Chance found it distasteful lying to the major. Even so, he knew he didn't dare share the story of his friendship and cooperation with an Indian the military was determined to recapture.

"Oh, I see, marshal. You needn't fear anything from Yellow Bear. He has already been recaptured."

Chance found himself a little disappointed by the news.

"Yellow Bear claimed he had a vision. In that vision, Marshal, he claimed that there was a dance that would transform them into an eagle. While still incarcerated, he began sharing this vision with others in the reservation."

"What was that, Major? Did you say an eagle dance?"

"Yes, marshal. Have you heard of this so-called Eagle Dance?"

"Not exactly, I haven't," Chance replied.

The major stopped his story long enough for a couple of passersby to continue down the street, out of earshot. Then he resumed.

"Yellow Bear was routinely stirring up the other braves, telling them about this Eagle Dance, which he claimed would make them all like him. And once they all became eagles, they would all be free to fly away to the mountains, away from the long knives, as he called us."

"If you don't mind me saying so, Major, it's sounds like you're taking the long way around the barn."

The major seemed to hesitate before he finished the story. "You have to understand, marshal, that at the time, the braves were talking of Eagle Dances and their plans to flee the reservation. Tensions were understandably high.

"We wanted to take Yellow Bear away to another location, so he could no longer incite the others. Upon seeing him being led away, the other Indians resisted, yelling, shouting, and pushing."

As Chance listened to the story, he hung his head, knowing there was no way this story was going to come out good for his friend, Yellow Bear.

"During the military inquest, I learned that a young private, much too green to be on that type of duty, said the pushing and shoving led to an accidental discharge of his weapon. Two other guards, upon hearing the shot, thought an escape was taking place. They opened fire as well.

"In the ensuing confusion, Yellow Bear, another brave, and his Indian wife were killed by the gun fire. Even our two finest surgeons did everything they could to save him. Later that afternoon, Yellow Bear died on the operating table."

Although he did his best to hide his reaction from the major, Chance was shaken by the news. His friend was dead, the man ultimately responsible for saving his life. He wondered how he would break this tragic news to Amy.

"Anyway, marshal, that is all I know about the renegade Arapaho," Major Witlow said. "Please pass the word along to your townspeople that they have nothing to fear from Yellow Bear. He is dead. So, if you'll please excuse me, Marshal, I'll rejoin my men now."

Chance was still reeling from the news when he saw the major climb back into the saddle. "Major, how many days ago did this all happen?" he shouted after him.

"Days?" Witlow said. "What are you talking about? Yellow Bear was killed over six months ago."

Chance just shook his head and started walking back towards the jail.

Author's Note

The washing away of Old West cemeteries by rains and flooding certainly isn't something which occurs only in the pages of this book. It was quite commonplace.

In fact, the washing away of grave markers is one of the main reasons we cannot forever lay to rest the persistent rumors that Billy the Kid was not really killed by Pat Garrett in 1881.

The grave markers of the Old Fort Sumner Cemetery (NM), where William Bonney was buried, were washed away in the 1904 flood. Due to this fact and poor record keeping of the time period, nobody can say with any degree of certainty where Billy's body is actually buried.

Even if the site of Billy the Kid's grave could be conclusively determined, and if DNA evidence proved it could be nobody other than him, there would still be individuals who persisted in the belief that the young outlaw escaped death at the hands of Pat Garrett.

It is these myths and legends that make the Old West a special and enduring place, unlike nothing else in world history. Perhaps that is why so many of us continue to love it so!

—R.G. Yoho

About the Author

R.G. Yoho is a West Virginia native with a passion for history and tales of the American West. Raised on a cattle farm, he is the prolific author of multiple Western novels, along with works of fiction and non-fiction. Yoho is a former president of the West Virginia Writers. Living with his wife near the banks of the Ohio River, Yoho is also a proud member of the Western Writers of America.

Now Available!
R.G. YOHO'S
ACTION/ADVENTURE WESTERNS

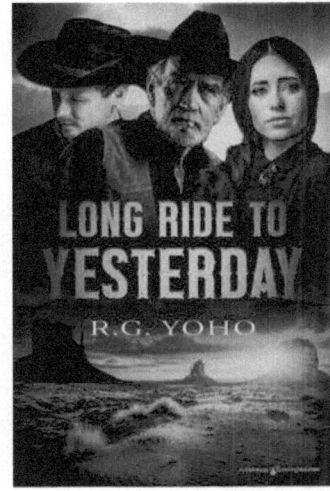

For more information
visit: www.SpeakingVolumes.us

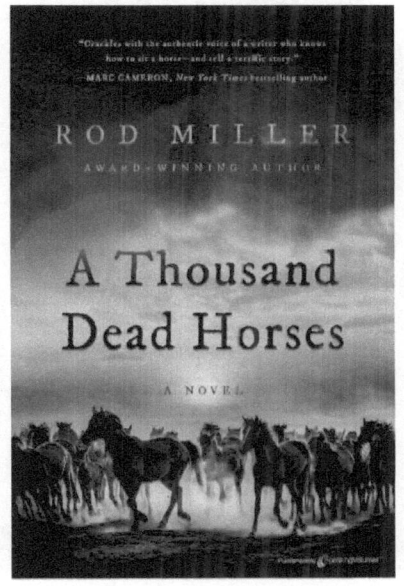

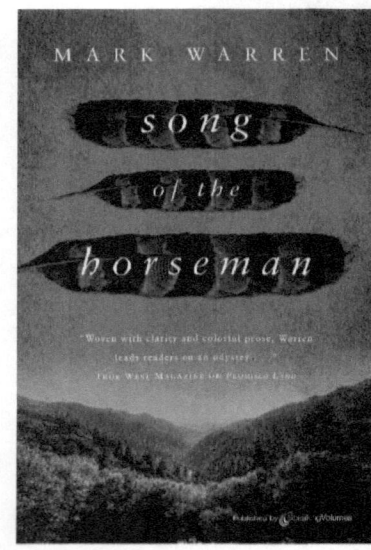